THE
Awakening
OF
GABBY DELANEY

KAT SCHAFER

authorHOUSE

AuthorHouse™
1663 Liberty Drive
Bloomington, IN 47403
www.authorhouse.com
Phone: 833-262-8899

Published by AuthorHouse 06/18/2021

ISBN: 978-1-6655-2985-3 (sc)
ISBN: 978-1-6655-2986-0 (hc)
ISBN: 978-1-6655-2987-7 (e)

Library of Congress Control Number: 2021912495

Print information available on the last page.

Any people depicted in stock imagery provided by Getty Images are models, and such images are being used for illustrative purposes only. Certain stock imagery © Getty Images.

This book is printed on acid-free paper.

One

The air was turning cool. Smells of fall seemed to be lingering everywhere. Children frolicking about on each corner. All of summer was coming to an end so the next season could make its grand entrance. The entire town of Woodland Grove loved and really got into the Fall Season. First, you have the high school football games where practically everyone attended. You either played on the team, support the team or you have a child who is currently on the team. Either way, high school football is your official start of the fall season.

Next, there's "the everything" Pumpkin craze. Where my mother personally adds her special touches here. She owns the only and of course, best bakery in Woodland, Jane Ann's. My mother and father were high school sweethearts. In fact, they've known each other since Kindergarten. Jake and Jane Ann Delaney are pretty much your perfect couple. They have two beautiful daughters. Myself of course, Gabby Delaney who will be turning seventeen this October by the way. And my younger sister Hadley who has just entered into her teen years at thirteen.

We live in a wonderful small town on a very lovely street. Each year every house is perfectly decorated for Halloween. The houses are filled with ghastly ghouls, hanging spiders, cobwebs, jack-o-lanterns, creepy costumes and candy galore. Really, our neighborhood is picture perfect. It's the first of September and it's the perfect time for everyone who is breathing to be decorating for all things Hallow. From simple down home fall decor to store bought creepy ghost galore. The town is done up to Halloween perfection. Going into my senior year this year.

Writing is my passion. I absolutely love to write. Anything from newspaper articles for the school paper to trying to get my first novel published. Quiet evenings around my house are hard to come by though so I usually head out to the local cemetery. Some find it creepy and weird but I actually enjoy my time there. Besides the fact that it's full of old history. It's really rather cool to hang out in such a dreary place. I find I do my best writing there. Things just seem to come to me as I sit leaned up against the old Oak tree. Time will just slip away as I'm writing. Stories and images just began to appear on the pages. Images in my head as if I'm seeing them right in front of my eyes.

For instance, right now I'm working on a story of young forbidden love. He's the bad boy type. Drives a 68 Camaro. Slick back hair, tight jeans and leather jacket. She's the preppy, shy quiet girl who gets good grades and wants to continue on with her education. They both come from two totally different families. But once their eyes met for the first time sitting at the Woodland Drive-in. Just feet apart. They immediately felt a connection. He was her dark dreamy guy that could take her away from it all. And she was the one good thing that would give him reason to living. Reason for breathing and hope for a better tomorrow. The only problem is that they come from two different worlds. It's pretty much frowned upon to enter into an unapproved love affair. But they didn't mind, not at all. Luella and Finn secretly met with one another every chance they got. Falling deeper in love with the other.

Until one cold, dark, rainy night when things just couldn't stay hidden any longer. Just as the two sat cuddled to each other in the back of Finn's Camaro. Luella's father had heard stories of his daughter's secret romance and decided that he would put a stop to it once and for all. He knows the spot the two lovers will be at and shows up with rifle in hand. The night became much darker and colder for Luella's father. After he ends poor Finn's life his daughter Luella grabs the gun from her father's hands and takes her own life. It left the small town in such shock and it sort of changed the way each saw one another. There were no sides from that time on. No matter where you were from or from what type of family. If you wanted to be friends with someone or date them, you could. But the tragic love story that turned out to be such horrible endings for them is still so very much a part of all the lives in that town. This story just appeared to me one evening as I sat in the old cemetery. Something seemed to catch my eye while I was adding the finishing touch to my story. A gravestone nearby. Looked very old. Could barely make out the writing but it looked, yes.

Just as I cleared away the Ivy and leaves, it read Finnley Harper. Strange coincidence I don't know, but it sure was quiet weird. Didn't know of any Harpers. Maybe my parents did. I'd ask them about the name when I get back home. But first, it was Friday night football and a boy that I've been hoping to talk to is the star quarterback. I know, how cliché of me, but it's not really my thing to go for the cool and popular ones. But this guy is different. Liam Carter has brown bouncy curls, big brown eyes and he truly is the sweetest. We end up doing some of the same projects together for interact.

Well, the interact club I'm in will do these special events and charities like big brother, big sister day. And the football players will help so they can get in extra credit for community work. Liam has been big brother to this adorable little seven year old named Chase. Chase lost his parents just a few years back to a house fire. He was lucky enough to have been with his grandmother that night. He was placed in her care but she also tragically passed away this last year to a massive heart attack. So this sweet quiet little boy now takes up residence at the Woodland Home for Children. He's been placed with Liam as big brother on Saturday or Sunday evening. I usually just make sure all the meals, rides, etc. are taken care of. So, I've gotten to know Liam and Chase a bit. He really is a different person when he's away from school and the rest of his gang.

So anyhow, I like to attend the football games for support and hoping that one day he'll wise up and see me. See me not as Gabby Delaney, the student, the buddy from Interact, but me. He'll want to get to know me ya know. And besides, even if he pays me no mind. I'll always have my guys there to keep me laughing. They really are the bestest friends anyone could ask for. There's my best friend since the third grade, Juliet and her boyfriend since the ninth grade Ezra. My homeboy and neighbor Abel. We've been friends since we could talk really.

Our parents have all been close friends. So no matter the party or reason, whatever happened usually involved us all. So, the games are always full of adventure. I show up a little late tonight but I manage to find them all sitting in our usual spot. Top row to the far right. Juliet is wearing her ever so happy smile and of course all decked out in our school colors, black and gold. They notice me as I turn to enter the stadium area.

"Up here" they're all yelling.

"It's about time" I get from Ezra.

"Yeah where ya been?" Juliet says. Abel then turns to me.

"I know, in the cemetery again. Working on being the next Stephen King". He says with a smile and a wink. I nod and just laugh it off to where I then direct my attention to the field. Everything seems to slow down and fade into silence. To where there's only one tall dreamy, brown eyed boy standing middle of a lonely field. I could run to him and declare my undying love for him. Or not, I could instead, sit here with my normal self, normal average friends and all the sounds of a Friday night football game come back into play. I'm at least happy that he knows my name. Knows that I do exist. It's better than nothing really. Game ends a little before ten that night. All of us plan on heading to the Woodland Drive-in to grab a burger and a shake. To my surprise Liam is parked next to us and he actually hollers over to us.

"Great game tonight huh?" he says while grabbing for his burger off the tray and taking a huge bite. We all look to one another as if we motion "us?" Is he actually talking to us?

"Yeah" I holler back while swallowing my sup of strawberry milkshake. He then smiles at me. We all finish our food and shakes and just hang around to talk awhile when I notice Liam getting out to throw away his trash. So I decide now is my moment. I'll approach him and just act casual. As I gather our car load of tonight's cuisine garbage I head out of the car and straight to the trash cans. Just as I reach Liam and barely get out a meek "hey".

Guess who then decides to join us? Yep, Liam's girlfriend Amiyah. Cute little perfect skin, perfect voice, body, hair, everything. Long blonde hair, blue eyes, cheerleader and wins everything that she ever enters. She comes bouncing on up, throws her hands around his waist from behind and says "Let's go. This place is starting to fill up with losers".

She throws a look my way and pulls him away. I could tell that he didn't appreciate her saying that but he couldn't say anything either. I needed to get through to him. I knew he had it in him to be a better person. He didn't really see titles and labels but being popular made him live a certain type of life. So when Saturday rolled around I thought I'd approach him again. Maybe he'd be himself with me and little Chase and maybe he'll get tired of living this popular life. After my eventful Friday was over and I head on home. Mom and dad were still up and sitting at the kitchen counter eating ice cream. So I decided to ask them about the Harper name. If they had known any growing up. We're all sitting there sharing laughs and talking about our day when I say "Oh, any of you guys ever hear of a Harper, Finnley Harper to be exact?" They both just stop suddenly and look at each other.

"Well?" I say to them. Mom says "no, why do you ask?"

"Oh come on. You guys gave each other a look when I said that name. You can't say it means nothing". I'm looking at them both.

"Dad? You were just as shocked. Sound familiar to you?" They both just start talking about other things. Trying to change the subject. I just shake it off and head up to say goodnight to my younger sister Hadley. She's lying on her bed, on her belly, feet up in the air, swinging and talking her friend's ear off on the phone. I guess they had an eventful day as well. I stroll by and head on inside her room.

"Boo" I say as I lean down to her. She turns to me with her usual big smile. Tells her phone friend that she'll talk with her later and immediately starts telling me about her day.

"Oh my gosh Gabs. I met that cutest boy today. He's so cute and has the coolest laugh" she says.

"Really?"

"Yeah, wait til you see him in person"

"So, what's his name?"

"Oh my gosh. That's cool too"

"What is? His name?" I ask.

"Yes" she says.

"His name is Emmett, Emmett Brown. You know, like from the movie?"

"The movie? Oh, Back to the Future?"

"Yeah, that one" she continues telling me all about this boy and how he just moved to town and was the cutest boy that my thirteen year old sister has ever laid eyes on. I had never seen my lil sis so happy, honestly. I wrap it up with her and turn in for the night. As I am lying in bed I can't take my mind off of that name, Finnley Harper. And the fact that both my parents seemed weirded out when I brought it up. I decided to hit the library Saturday morning before I had to meet with my interact club. I was determined to find out more on this mysterious name. I started looking up old articles on the computer and reading through old town history books. I came across old high school yearbooks that had some pictures of a dark haired young man named Finn Harper. Tight pants, jean jacket and slick back hair. Almost like I had pictured him for my book. But I had never been told any stories of any kind with anyone that even remotely resembled this man. I kept scrolling and reading and to my amazement, there it was. Right in front of me. A picture of Jake Delaney, Jane Ann Jackson and Finn Harper. All smiles and sitting at a picnic table outside at school. Both my parents with Finn. So they definitely knew him, and more importantly. Why and how was I imagining this man for my book? I had so much on my mind. So much to figure out. I decided on skipping interact today and of course my chance to talk with Liam. I had to know what the secret was about this man. I'll visit mom at work at the diner. Maybe she'll give me some answers with dad not around. It's usually pretty busy on the weekends. Especially this time of year. As I enter she immediately notices me and motions for me to come to her.

"Here" she says as she pushes an apron my way.

"I have never been so happy to see you in my life" she says then smiles.

"If you could help out for just a couple of hours. I'd owe you big time" I figured I could use this to my advantage. After a few hours maybe I could get some answers from her about Finn and why they're being so mysterious. So, of course I stay and help. Put in my time and after about four and a half hours later we get a moment of peace. It's finally starting to settle down and people are clearing out. I'm wiping my last table when mom comes over to me with a piece of her famous pumpkin bread and mocha latte.

"I can't thank you enough, really" she says as we both sit and enjoy our hard earned desserts.

"Monica quit today. She says something about she's going nowhere in this one horse town, and that she had to get out now and fast. She literally walked in, handed me her name tag and left me hanging. Then a bus of elders that, I guess are traveling across America stops in. And don't get me wrong, I love customers and I love my diner, but today was very trying for me".

"Mom, not to interrupt but since you now owe me. How about you answer one question?"

"Well that was fast"

"Finn Harper, who was he? And don't tell me you don't know or that you've never heard of him. I looked him up at the library and I saw a picture in an old yearbook with him, you and dad. And you guys looked very much like you knew each other." We both sat for a moment looking at one another. She looks out the window for a moment then turns back to me, and begins.

"He was a wonderful young man. Smart, hard working and very talented. He was a good friend of your fathers"

"What happened? Why be so secretive about him?"

"We grew up in a different time. Woodland Grove was not always like you see it now. People weren't always as accepting of one another"

"What do you mean? That was only like twenty years or so ago"

"I know dear but things were so very different at that time" She continues telling me how depending on what you wore, who you knew, who your parents were, even your last name made a difference in where you fit in. But she's talking like it was so long ago, not just twenty years. The Harper family never really had much. They worked hard, some of them did. But they never really got that far in life. They were judged by just their last name.

"You see honey, I had a good friend that I had known practically all through school. Her name was Luella" Just as that name comes out I immediately felt confused, shocked and a little creeped out. How did I know these names? Why was I writing about them? I sit up closer to the table. Trying to take this all in as my mother is still going on with her story. But I didn't hear anything past Luella.

"Wait, Mom. So you're telling me, that in your time, in high school, you knew of a Luella and a Finn?"

"Yeah, in fact they were" I had to interrupt.

"They were together, weren't they?" I say then turn to my bag to pull out my notebook. I place it on the table.

"It's in here"

"What is?" she asks.

"Those names. The fact that they were a couple. I wrote about it" she's looking at me, all confused.

"OK"

"No Mom. I wrote about it all Summer. In fact, I started this book last year. Way before I ever heard of these two names". We both look at each other. All puzzled for a bit. Mom sits back in her seat and I could tell is trying to make sense of all this.

"But how could I know? I mean, what are the odds of me putting those two names together?" It's getting really interesting and I'm barely able to stay seated.

"Wait, did something bad happen to Finn, or both maybe?" I'm asking her.

"Actually yeah. They were both killed our last year in high school. Wait, what do you have in your book bout them?"

"It was a love that could never be and Luella's father kills Finn and then" She stops me to add.

"Then she takes her father's gun and kills herself?" We're both sitting up and remaining quiet. Of course taking it all in here. Then I relax my body back into my seat.

"This is really creepy and honestly I'm not sure that I want to know the rest." All this was just too much for a seventeen-year-old small town girl. Maybe I had heard my parents at some point talking about them and that's where I got the names. But then, how would I know that both their lives were taken? From that moment on, my life would never be the same. Cute boy in high school. Making good grades on my last test. It all seemed so little any more. Something bigger was happening. Something bigger was about to come into my life and change everything.

Two

The weekend had flew by and before I knew it I was standing in the hallway, in front of what appeared to be a carpentry class. As I'm standing there looking in I could see I could see a boy, looked about seventeen. Kinda like he was way outdated with his tight jeans and leather jacket. Looks to be working on a birdhouse. He's standing there blowing away the excess wood shavings and checking out his completed work. When he notices me watching him. I kinda give him a half smile and wave. Figured I already looked creepy enough. He smiles back and holds up his work. Like, look what I did. He seemed to be proud so I gave him the "not bad" nod and grin. The bell rings and I realize I'm late for my Creative Writing Class. I make my way on over to my desk and notice, there's a new girl sitting beside me. Hair all tight and curled, in a ponytail. Pink polo with, is that a poodle skirt? I do believe it was. She looks my way, smiles. Then quietly begins to introduce herself.

"I'm Luella. Just transferred to this class" Yep, you heard right, Luella. I take a hard swallow.

"Luella? was that it?" I ask.

"Yeah it's a family name. Handed down from all the great women before me. Or so my dad says". OK I was starting to feel like I was being punked or something. So I start laughing a little.

"Who put you up to this?"

"Up to what?" she ask.

"Was it my mother? I know, it was Abel. He's always trying to trick me or something. I'd bet him and mom are in this together". I just decide to let it go and I'd figure this out after class. After all, this was my only class for today and I'd have time to get to the bottom of this later.

I wanted to learn more about Finn and Luella so I headed back to the local library after school. There had to be more on what happened that night if they really were both killed. First article I come across is a chili cook off and couples dance. Mom and dad would have been about my age, seventeen. Says here that Jake Delaney won first place for the cook off and won five hundred dollars. Wow, that's pretty awesome. Second place went to Finnley Harper where he received a year supply of chili from the Green Mountain Chili Company. Not as nice as the first but still a win. I keep scrolling to find an arrest file on my dad. It was him and Finn. Got into a scuffle at the bowling ailey but my dad was let go and Finn had to do twenty-four hours in jail and forty-eight hours community service. Didn't give much info so I'll have to talk with dad about this one. I guess I got so into my reading and never noticed that the place was completely empty. I couldn't even find Ms. Mary the librarian. Strange. I then notice a small noise coming from the back. Around the fiction section. Of course I'm going to nosey around to see who or what it was. I turn the corner and notice a couple making out.

"Oh, I'm sorry" I say then begin to turn around. But I couldn't help but notice the boy looked just like the one from carpentry class. And come to think of it, he also looked a whole lot like Finn from those articles.

"You" I say and motion toward him.

"Me" he says. And of course gives me that same gorgeous smile.

"Aren't you the one from school earlier? You had the Bird house"

You got it" he says. And the girl, she was the one who introduced herself to me in my writing class as Luella. I just step back a moment.

"What's going on?" The boy walks closer to me.

"We've been waiting til you were ready Gabby" he says.

"Ready for what? And how do you know my name?" As I'm slowly stepping backwards away from them. He continues walking closer to me.

"I've been visiting you for a while now. First, I came to you and sat with you while you leaned up against that old oak tree in the cemetery. I realized who you were and saw that your heart and mind were open." He continues getting closer as I'm trying to inch away more. When my back comes to a halt at the horror section.

"What do you mean open?"

"Not many can see us, and it took a while for you. But you could hear us, feel us and you could connect with us in your mind."

"I don't understand"

"It's OK. You will, in time. I gave you your story. I gave you the words to put onto paper. Now you just gotta finish it for us"

"Finish it, how?"

"You can't find what you're looking for, can you?"

"And what's that?" I asked.

"You want to know the truth. You want to know the story of what happened to me and Luella"

"I've been reading and it's not there. My mother told me something about you guys getting killed, but no other details"

"And you won't find it or even get it from anyone in town. They are all hiding the truth"

"The truth? Why?"

"Because it's too hard for them to accept. They want to keep Woodland Grove as perfect as they can"

"What is the truth?" I ask. But a voice comes from the front of the library.

"Miss, are you OK? I really need to be closing up now" It was Ms. Mary hollering back at me. I turn to her and motion as to give me a minute, then back his way. There was no one there. I searched around the corners but it was empty. Just me and Ms. Mary. Thoughts were rushing through my head. What was going on and why was I the one they had picked? I admit, I was curious. I went straight to the diner when I had left the library.

"Mom" I say as I enter. She's standing behind the counter talking to Sheriff Cody and Deputy Wyatt. "Mom" I say again as they all turn my way.

"What is it child? Can't you see I'm busy?" She says while pouring the sheriff another cup of coffee. I lean in close to her and quietly tell her "We have to talk" She directs her attention toward the sheriff and his deputy and says "You'll have to excuse me fellas" "Of course" the sheriff says then sips on his coffee. We walk to the back and I can't even put it all into words. I'm excited, anxious and also a bit nervous about telling her. Fearing that she'll never believe me. I mean, who would? It's not like it's everyday a person gets approached by a, what do I even call him? Ghost, dead person, spirit? Either way, you don't hear of people coming back from the dead to talk to a normal human being.

"Calm down Gabby. What is it?"

"OK Mom" I say then take a deep breath. "I want you to fully listen to what I have to tell you before you say or do anything. Don't even think. Just listen."

"Sure Gabby. Go ahead" So I begin telling her all about how I first saw what I'm assuming is Finn at school, also Luella. Then they approached me at the library to where he then tells me of how I have to tell his story, or hear the truth. Something like that. This is where she immediately stops me.

"Are you sure? I mean, are you sure of their names and who they were?"

"Yeah Mom. I'm pretty sure. Plus he looked just like the photo from the yearbook. He was saying I won't find the truth because the town is hiding it. It wants to stay perfect. What's he talking about?" She takes me by the shoulders and tells me in the most stern voice I've ever heard from her.

"You listen to me. I want you to go straight home and stay there. Stop all this nonsense, Now."

"But Mom"

"No Gabriella. You don't know what you're messing with here. All this was left in the past and it needs to stay there. Now get on home and not a word of this to anyone, especially your father" We stood silent. I had just saw true terror in my mothers eyes for the first time and I wasn't sure what to do about it. As I was fixing to leave the diner I looked to Sheriff Cody and he had a strange look of danger and fear. It's like he was warning me. I took the long walk home that day and decided to go by the cemetery. I walked through to see if I could get a feel or something. I took my time going through each tombstone. Looking for Luella's name I guess, but I didn't find it. Took a moment to maybe say a word or talk to Finn. Hoping that he could hear me or give me some type of advice on what to do. "I don't know if you can hear me right now or if this is really your gravestone, but I really need some type of help here. I don't know why you came to me. I don't know what you want but I'll try to help if you'll just give me some type of advice here. Some more information on what it is exactly that I'm suppose to be doing. I mean, my mother was not happy at all when I mentioned you and now that you've came to me in person. Well, she's really not" And that's when he approaches me again.

"You told your mom?" I turn to him as he comes from behind the tree.

"Yeah, she was not happy" I say.

"No, I'd say not"

"Why? Why would my mom care if I helped you? I thought you all use to be friends"

"Is that what she told you?"

"Yeah. Plus I saw a photo in the high school yearbook. It was you, my mom, my dad. Everyone seemed fine. All smiles."

"Well we were at first, friends. I thought the world of your mother. And your father, he was a good guy"

"But?"

"But, two sides here. We live on opposite sides of the track"

"Yeah, what is it with that? Mom kept saying something like that"

"My family didn't have much. My old man worked his ass off day and night to provide for us. My mom got sick as soon as I entered high school. She had cancer. She put on a brave face and tried to muscle through but my last year of school she really turned for the worse. It took everything in her just to sit up in bed. My old man worked so hard doing anything he could just to pay the bills and feed us kids. It was breaking him down watching my mother getting weaker and losing all her hair and weight. She was so frail but still so beautiful. She's the only one my old man ever loved."

"I'm so sorry Finn"

"When she finally passed away, the old man left. Figured he just couldn't bare it any longer. So I had to take care of my younger sisters and brothers. They were all too young to work so I took on whatever side job I could get just to feed them. I thought I lucked out when I entered this contest. The first place winner would get Five hundred dollars and we could have used that."

"I read about that, but that you came in second to my dad" I felt so sad for him. Like it was sorda my fault.

"Yeah, Jake knew what winning meant for me. He knew and he still entered and won"

"But my dad's not like that. Did he know about your mom and how you needed the money?"

"He knew"

"I'm sure there was some reason"

"There was. He wanted to impress a girl. Your mom"

"There has to be some kind of mistake or a reason to why"

"That is the reason. That's why. He couldn't get her to talk to him after he had got caught kissing another girl. She was interested in the cook off and he found out. I asked him, begged him not to enter. I needed to win that money. I even asked him what he was going to do with it. Kinda hoping he would give it to me, but he didn't"

"So all this over a stupid contest?"

"No. The contest was the beginning. I couldn't let it go and was upset later that night. When I saw your mom and dad at the Bowling Ailey I lost it. But I never swung on him. He kept coming at me. Trying to look big in front of everyone. He pushed me backwards and I still didn't do anything. Except get up and try to walk away. But your dad wouldn't stop. He came at me again. Only this time he came swinging. I got a lick or two in but your dad really did a number on me"

"That's horrible. Are you sure it was my father? I can't see him dong anything like that"

"I was taken away to spend the night in jail and got community service for it. Your dad" He says while shaking his head.

"Nothing. He was told to go home"

"Seriously. Why, I mean how? That don't seem to be very fair"

"No it don't does it? But that's how it was. Different tracks"

"So your saying my dad got away with it cause he was different than you, better?"

"Something like that"

"That's just horrible. But the town is nothing like that now"

"Isn't it?"

"I don't see it that way"

"Don't you? Why haven't you asked out your quarterback yet? What are you waiting for?"

"That's different"

"How? Different sides of the track"

It took me a second but he was right. Things were still like that. My friends and I sit in our "normal average Joe" seats while the popular ones always do their thing. And Liam will only treat me as an equal when we're not around his friends. And here I am trying so hard to get his attention. But I've been right in front of him the whole time. If he can't see and accept me already then I don't think I want him ever to. I had a lot to think on that night. Who were my parents really? My dad has always helped anyone whenever he could. Same with my mom. She gives more food away at the diner then I think she ever sells. And Liam, I'm trying to make him someone he's not. If he was truly interested in me and wanted to ask me out then he would. But he hasn't and probably never will. All because we are different. Guess you could say we come from different sides of the tracks as well. Not anymore. I'm not giving any worry to people who are just like me. We breath the same air. Walk the same streets. Take in the same bullcrap from the guy behind us. Starting tomorrow, Gabby Delaney will walk her own walk. Strut her own stuff. The town of Woodland is about to get a makeover. Before going home that night I made a quick stop to the grocery store. Had a few items that I needed to pick up. Like I said, tomorrow morning will start a new era for Gabby. Set my alarm a little earlier that morning. Big plans and I couldn't wait to get them started.

As I roll into Woodland High. Sunglasses shadin' all the haters. Ripped jeans, torn motley crue shirt and are you ready for the grand finale? Purple and teal hair. This will definitely set some boundaries. Talk about two sides of the track. Well Woodland, Gabby Delaney is merging to the left. Setting her own side. I left early so I didn't have time for any of my family to see the new look and get their wonderful opinions, but I'm sure I'll be getting plenty here. First to really get my eye, Juliet. She almost drops her books in hand and drops her jaw.

"Gabby?" She says in a way of wonder.

"Sure is. What do you think?" I say and give myself a spin.

"Are you OK?" she asks.

"OK? I've never felt better" I really hadn't either. I was so confident about my new look. I didn't care what others were gonna think. Abel then comes around the corner.

"Woah. Is there some sort of costume party I missed out on?"

"Nope. This is my new look. How do you like it?" I ask. He steps back as to take it all in. Gives me a spin and a look over and then shakes his head to a Yes.

"I like it. I do. I mean, maybe stick to one color for the hair, but I'm really digging the purple and those ripped jeans" I was really feeling my new move. I mean, I was practically making a statement here. Which was, I didn't care what you thought of me. I like me and I'm loving how I'm looking right now. I was so wrapped up in myself and showing off to my friends that I had completely forgotten about Liam and his friends. But don't worry, Amiyah will make sure that I get her full opinion on my new ensemble. All I could hear from behind me, approaching. A gasp of wasted air. As she throws her hand over her mouth and stops as though her feet were caught in glue. All I heard was giggles at first, then "Oh.....My.....Gosh!!! She has totally lost it this time. I mean, did your little sister dress you today? Or you lose a bet for this one?" She says then turns toward her goon squad to get their reaction. You know, making sure they were laughing in harmony with herself. I smile and nod it off. Knowing I'm way better than this. Or to even give in to her childish acts. I look over to Liam to see his reaction. He's a little taken at first. Looked as though he was stuck in the middle, but which way would he go here? Now was the time to stand up and show you could be a decent person. Show you're not like Amiyah and the rest. But he chose wrong. He looked Amiyah's way, laughed along with them then back my way.

"Really Gab. Halloween is next month. Getting a jump start?" They all continue laughing then make their way down the hall. That day was a turning point for me. I was more set in my ways of keeping this new style now and I had seen Liam for who he really was. Went through the rest of my school day like a charm. Most were accepting of my wardrobe and even decided on going with how they wanted to dress from then on. It gave them the courage to be themselves. My parents were a little freaked out about it, at first. They wanted me to change back but we met in the middle. I kept my clothes of choice but went back to my usual brown hair. With a few hints of color here and there. Couple of weeks had passed and I hadn't heard nor saw Finn or Luella. Hadn't even brought it back up to my parents. Figured maybe it was all over since I had seen the light with Liam. It was almost October and getting closer to my favorite holiday. The air was getting much cooler and the streets were getting filled with leaves everywhere. It was picture perfect. It was a perfect day for writing I thought. So I headed out to the cemetery to have some quiet and alone time. Got settled in at my usual spot by the tree. Took out my notebook and began jotting down ideas for a new book. I hadn't wrote about Finn and Luella since I last saw them. Different ideas were coming to mind but nothing really stuck out. Then I could hear some humming from behind me. I turn to see who it was. It was Finn.

"Hey, Where have you been? I thought I'd never see you again"

"I've been here" he says.

"Where's Luella? Isn't she with you?"

"Nah. She never really sticks around"

"Well what do you do here all day? I mean, do you just sit here all alone?"

"I'm around" he says then gets up and starts slowly walking by his gravestone.

"I've been keeping an eye on you"

"Really, Why?"

"You know, just to make sure you're OK. And, I still need you to do something for me"

"You said that before. The truth?"

"Yeah. It has to be done Gabby so I can leave here"

"Leave, here? The graveyard or Earth?" He smiles at me.

"Sometimes you remind me of your mother" He says then pushes back my hair.

"You never really told me what I'm supposed to do exactly"

"Didn't I?"

"Not really"

"I told you of how your father betrayed me. How his kind got away with whatever, but my kind had to pay"

"Yeah, but are you saying you want me to make my dad pay somehow?"

"It has to happen Gabs" he says while turning his voice a little deeper and colder.

"By the way" he says. "I love the new look. In fact, that's why I stayed away for a while. You made a statement. Showed you didn't care what others thought. You separated yourself from Woodland. Became your own person"

"But I don't know how to make him pay. I could get him to admit he done wrong"

"No"

"But that'll help"

"It'll do nothing. He has to pay for all his crimes. Just like I did"

"All his crimes. What else is there?"

"Go to him. Go to your father and ask him again, about me. Ask him what really happened". I looked down for a second then back up and he was gone. OK, I've got to get to the bottom of this. I decided this time to go straight to my father, not my mom. I was going to get some answers. I Headed over to the furniture store where dad works. He'll be on break soon and I think it's time for a father daughter lunch date.

"Dad" I say with a smile and holding a bag of burgers and fries from the diner.

"Good. I'm starved" he says then walks my way.

"Let's eat out on the patio" He motions to head ouside.

"So I've been working on my writing again" I say to him while munching a bite of burger.

"Cool. What's it about?"

"It's about a forbidden love set back about twenty years or so ago"

"Sounds cool. How's it coming?"

"Well I've hit a snag"

"Snag?"

"Yeah, I'm kinda stuck on where to go with it. I mean it could be finished where I'm at now, but it don't feel done"

"Why don't you ask your mom for some help? After all, She'll know a lot about the seventy's"

"Well I did. I mean, I talked to her some about what's in my book. But you see, she don't agree with it"

"Don't agree, why's that?"

"Well it's not really what my book's about more than who it's about"

"Well who is it about? Don't tell me you decided to come up with some crazy story about us"

"No, at least I didn't think that you guys were a part of it. Not at first"

"But?"

"Well, when I mentioned to her some names, she told me to never speak of them again" He then almost chokes on his food. Placing his burger down he then asks me "It's not about this Finn character again is it?"

"Yeah Dad, it is. Him and Luella"

"Where are you even getting these names from? Did your mother tell you something?"

"That's just it. They just came to me when I was writing. In fact, my whole story just came to me as I was sitting in the cemetery"

"I think we're done here" he says then pushes away from the table.

"Dad, you have to tell me what happened" He stops before going inside and turns to me.

"You don't know the half of it, and it would be in your best interest to leave this alone" he says then heads on in. No, this is not going to happen like this. I want, I need answers. I pull open the door and yell back to him just before he reaches the office door.

"What did you do Dad?" He stops, never turning my way. Never looking at me.

"Go home Gabby. We'll talk about it there" he says then shuts the door behind him. What exactly did my parents do? What were they hiding? I tried to cope with all this. Days went by, even weeks. My parents and I hardly spoke. I never asked again or even mentioned their names. Just two more weeks til Halloween. I tried to make the most of my favorite holiday season. Spent nights out with my friends. Even met some new kids that lived just outside of Woodland, over in the next town, George Town. Chrissy, who is eighteen and a high school dropout. Cool person though. Cute petite, pixie cut blonde hair and a few piercings here and there. Her cousin Pain. Actual name is Henry but loves the feel of pain. Has broke most his bones throughout childhood. About the same age. Also a dropout. And his girlfriend Willow. Kinda dark, scary looking. Jet black hair, tattoos, piercings and believes she's a witch. But other than that she's actually very friendly. Came across them in the cemetery one evening. I'm sitting there, doing my writing when they come strolling through. Kinda odd to see new visitors, especially in the cemetery. Chrissy was the first to approach me.

"Hey" she says while kinda tip toeing around the area. I look up from my notebook to a petite blonde girl smiling down at me.

"Hey"

"So whatcha doin' here? I mean, someone die recently or something?" she ask.

"No. I just come here a lot"

"Really? Why?"

"Oddly, it's kinda nice. It's quiet and I come here to write and think"

"Oh, that's cool" she says then skips around the tree. Popping her head back around she says "I'm Chrissy by the way"

"Hi! Gabby"

"Gabby. That's a cool name"

"Actually it's Gabriella but I can't stand that. So it's just Gabby" Just then the other two appear.

"Oh, this is my cousin Pain and his girlfriend Willow" she says. We're all looking at one another. Exchanging our heys.

"So Pain, Why that name?" I ask.

"Cause he's stupid" Chrissy replies. He looks her way and gives her the finger.

"Cause I feel no pain. I mean, I enjoy pain. It don't affect me. Really" he says then rams his fist against his head. When his girlfriend Willow comes in "Stop it. You're seriously gonna do some damage one day" she says. They gaze at one another then immediately start making out.

"Gross you guys" Chrissy says while making the gag motion.

"Come on" she takes me by the arm then says "Let's me and you get acquainted" We walk away from the loving couple.

"So where you from?" I ask.

"I mean I don't think I've ever seen you guys around here"

"No, you probably haven't. That's cause we're from George Town."

"Well what brings you this way?"

"Bored. We've seen everything there is to see in George so figured we'd come over here"

"Not much to see here" I tell her.

"Yeah. We were thinking the same. Actually we were heading out when Willow saw this old cemetery and wanted to stop"

"Well I'm glad you did. Kinda nice to see new faces around here"

That was the start of a long wonderful friendship for me and Chrissy. Spent my weeks before Halloween with my new buds and it really helped take my mind off my parents and this Finn business. But by Halloween night things had come to a halt. Finn visited me again and demanded that I make this right or things would get really nasty. In fact, time was up. Something had to be fixed and made right by tonight or else Finn would be forced to take action.

Three

I'm seeing a darker side of Finn now and starting to feel a bit freightened for my parents. What did he mean by take action? And what could I do to make all this right? Time was up. So I had to get my Dad to talk. Big Halloween bash tonight. The whole town will be attending. If anything was gonna happen, it had to be now. So I head home to find both my parents there. Getting ready for the big bash tonight. I decided that they were going to tell me the whole truth and that all this would be finished tonight. I head on in and find mom first in the kitchen. Pouring herself an early cocktail.

"Hittin' the juice a little early today mom?" I say as I walk on up to her standing by the counter.

"Good. You're gonna need it for what I'm about to say"

"Oh Gabby, quit being so dramatic"

"Dramatic Mom? No, this is nothing. Dramatic hasn't even shown its ugly face yet"

"Honestly Gab. It's Halloween. Do you really wanna ruin the night? You know this is everyones favorite event"

"Ruin it? Well now, that depends on you and dad doesn't it?"

"Gabby, just say what it is and get it over with" She says while pouring another drink.

"OK Mother. I know that things didn't go so well for you, my father and Finn"

"Really Gabriella? Not this again"

"Really Mother. Dad wasn't very nice to Finn and it was really bullcrap that he let him go down during that fallout at the Bowling Alley"

"Enough Gabby. I'm not listening to any of this" she says as she tries to turn and leave the room. But something inside of me couldn't take it any longer. I had had enough of them not listening to me and treating me like a child. All I felt was anger and that she wasn't going to leave the room. She stopped in her tracks. She literally was froze to that spot.

"What's going on?" she says in a state of panic.

"Why can't I move?" I walk over to her. Just as surprised as she was. Not really knowing how or what was keeping her there. I walk around to look her in the face.

"Now you will listen to me Mom. You'll sit down" her body then moves backwards to place herself on the stool at the counter. I walk on over.

"You'll sit here and listen. Then, you're going to answer my questions" I say then smile to her, but in a creepy way. This is when dad makes his entrance.

"Jake, something's wrong" she tells him.

"She's doing something to me"

"What are you talking about Jane Ann?" he says while trying to continue on with what he was doing. Which was trying to pour himself a cup of coffee.

"Dad" I say while smiling of course.

"Won't you join us?" just then his body moves over to sit next to mom.

"What the hell?" he says as his body is placed on the stool.

"Good. Now we can start" I say but rudely get interrupted by my father.

"What the hell is going on here? Why can't I move? How are you doing this?"

"I told you she was doing something" mom says.

"Mom, Dad. Something has been brought to my attention. Finn" And I of course am interrupted once again.

"Finn bullshit. I'm tired of hearing his damn name" dad says. I smile, take a deep breath, then continue.

"Finn has come to me and told me some things"

"Come to you? What are you talking about Gabby?"

"Dad, if you will quit interrupting me. I will get to all that. Now, sit there and BE SILENT" I say sternly. They both zip up quick and not a word comes out.

"There, that's better. Now, as I was saying. I have been contacted by a sweet young man who has informed me that some terrible things happened long ago, and that he would like them fixed. I guess you could say fixed. Either way, seems that you weren't so friendly growing up dad. Now why's that?" He looks at me then starts to reply.

"Oh never mind. No worry. We're going to fix it now. Aren't we?" I say as I look to both.

"Gabby, honey. Your father did nothing wrong. Finn wasn't a good kid"

"Mom, mother" I say to get her to stop talking.

"I figured you would try to take dads side so I'm gonna need you to hush. Just sit there and listen. I'm sure dad will change your mind." I look to my father.

"Go ahead daddy. Let's hear your side. But this time, let's hear the truth, all of it. It's getting late and we really don't wanna miss the big party now do we?" He looks to my mother then back to me.

"I said the truth" I felt that in my core. It's as if he couldn't lie. Everything that came out that night was what really happened. What Finn wanted to get out. He looks at me and begins. It's pretty much all the same until he gets to the part where, instead of Finn and Luella cuddled up in the back of Finn's car my dad had done the unthinkable. You see, since my mom had caught him cheating, she was angry with my dad. She didn't really let him back in so he went out that night. Halloween night to be exact. He went out, got drunk and was looking for company. When he comes across Luella. She had just gotten off work from the local diner and was walking home. He offered to give her a ride. At first, she was hesitate but since she knew who my father was she accepted. They drive out to the old barn house to where he forced himself on poor Luella. He pushed her out and told her to never speak of this to anyone. If she told, then he would murder her whole family. All this didn't seem to shock my mother. It's as though she already knew.

"Mom. You don't look surprised" I say.

"Gabriella you've heard enough. Stop this now"

"But mother, I feel like there's more to hear" I turn to my father.

"Keep going dad" It was all shocking. I began to see why Finn wanted all this made right.

"Dad, go on" He begins to cry.

"I said continue"

"I was drinking then and I wasn't myself. Gabby honey. I have hated myself for what I done"

"But why didn't you ever apologize or do anything about it?"

"I never got the chance. That was the same night that Luella's father shot Finn and she killed herself" They both sat there crying. I felt as if I didn't know who my parents were.

"And you knew mom?" I get closer to her and louder.

"You knew this whole time. You never did or said anything either. You two let the whole town think horrible of Finn. Like he was some kind of monster. When all he was trying to do was feed his siblings. Be a good person and boyfriend. Luella saw the good. She saw him for who he was and loved him.

"You don't understand Gabby"

"Really mom. What don't I understand?"

"It was a different time then. We were just trying to make something of ourselves"

"Yeah, so was Finn. Dad you let him go to jail for your stupidity and even took money from him. Practically food from his mouth"

"He came in second and won food for a year"

"Yeah, you guys amaze me. You sit here in your fancy house. Perfect lives, family, children. Acting like you have it all, but really you stole it."

"Gabby come on"

"No dad" both are still stuck seated and probably still wondering how it's all happening. Honestly, I'm still wondering how it's all happening. I'm figuring it's Finn helping me. The truth is all he wanted and now he's got it. Just then he appears to me, this time in my kitchen. He places his hand on my shoulder. It startles me a moment. As I turn to him I could see he felt at peace now.

"It's done Gabby" he says.

"Done? it's still not fair that this town thinks you're trash" Both my parents look at me then to each other.

"Gabby, who are you talking to?" mom says. I look at Finn then at her.

"That's right, you can't see him" I say.

"See who? Finn, is it Finn that you're talking to?" mom asks.

"Yeah mom. I told you. Been telling you for a while now but you wouldn't listen"

"Honey I'm sorry. I just didn't know what to say"

"It's fine mom, really. Now all dad as to do is go to the party tonight and tell everyone what he did. Then, this can all be over"

"Don't be silly. They'll never listen nor would they care"

"Well we can make them listen" I say.

"Can't we" Finn tells me that he is at peace with the fact that it is finally out, but dad had to be punished.

"Punished? How? How far does this have to go?" I ask. My parents try to gather themselves and continue to get ready for the big bash. They try to act as if what just happened, didn't. Thankfully, my sister Hadley was at a friend's house. Don't think I'm ready to explain all this to her. On the bright side, I invited my new buds to come along for our big Halloween bash. Abel will be DJ'ing it tonight. Haven't had much time with him lately so I'm trying to get in a few hours before we all have to leave. I run next door to his house for a few moments of normal before tonight. He's looking ever so handsome dressed as the Joker. One of his favorite characters. I'll be going as a dark witch of the night. I felt it was ever so fitting. We got in a few moments of good conversation. It felt nice. Laying there on his bed, just like old times. Listening to The Doors, a favorite of his as well. Just getting caught up on our day to day. I turn to him before I head out.

"You know I love you Abel. Always have. Always will" Smile then head out. I wasn't for sure what was gonna happen tonight. All I knew is that it was more than likely going to turn out nasty. I really thought someone could die.

Four

Here I stand looking all cute in my witch costume. Long black hair, pale skin, spiders on my face, super short mini skirt, black heeled thigh high boots, long pointy black nails. I'm telling you I was pretty awesome. Still hadn't figured out if it was me or Finn working through me but what happened at the house was pretty amazing. It's like I could feel it. I wanted my mother to sit down so she did, and the same with my dad. Was it magic? I'm just not sure but I did enjoy the power. I'm standing right smack in the middle of town. Right under the huge banner that read Twenty-Fifth Annual Halloween Bash. Welcome Everyone. Get it? Bats, Vampires. Anyhow, standing there next to a huge marshmallow man or whatever he was, waiting for my parents to arrive. Looking down at my watch, it should be any minute now. Sure enough there they come. Just turning the corner by the muffin stand and the apple picking contest. How fitting, Bonnie and Clyde. Mom walks on up to me while dad starts to work the crowd.

"How cute and fitting for the couple" I say to her with a smirk. Mom leans in closer to me.

"I'm not sure what you're expecting here tonight Gabby, but I've worked hard to get to where I am and I'm not about to lose it over something so, well, pointless" she says then turns to walk away. So, that's how you want to play it then? Apparently they're not worried about what could happen or even remember earlier at the house. I took in a breath of fresh air, closed my eyes and I remember my fists closing and it felt cold and dark. I opened up my eyes and sat sights on my mother. I could pick her out so easily. As if no one else were there. A voice from deep within came out of me.

"MOTHER" I said. It traveled across the crowd and found my mother. She turned ever so slowly to look at her daughters face.

"We have things to do" I say then smiled her way.

"Now go get father, and bring him here" I turned my head slowly toward a gazebo and pointed in that direction.

"And mother, I'll be waiting, do hurry back" My mother couldn't resist doing as I instructed her to. It was like earlier. She would go get father and bring him to me. I waited patiently for them to return and while waiting I saw Chrissy, Pain and Willow. They stopped by, said hey. Willow wanted to show off a trick she had learned. Guess it was supposed to be like a spell. She would make these marbles spin around that she was holding in her hand. She held out both her hands. Placed three marbles in each and begin chanting something. It was something like; In my hand I hold is mine. Taking turning around in time. In my hand I hold is mine. Taking turning around in time. After that they seemed to spin a bit. Neat and cool but not totally awesome. I looked at her after, gave her my famous half smile then said "That's cute. Watch this" I focused my attention on the gazebo lights dangling around the top. I made them flash then all the Jack-O-Lanterns were changing color in light and some had smoke coming from them. They looked at me in amazement.

"How are you doing this?" Chrissy asked. I continue changing lights that were strung through town and adding touches to the decor. At this point, I'm no longer surprised. Just enjoying the fact that I can do all these things. Mother and father came hand in hand. Looking as though they have all this figured out. They stop just as they reach the steps to the gazebo. I'm standing just at the top.

"Dad" I say. "Are you ready?"

"What is it that you're wanting me to do Gabby?"

"Simple. Just tell the truth. The story of what you done wrong. You have to make it right" He stands there a moment. Fighting the urge that I've laid upon him, to get up on the gazebo and speak those words.

"You can't fight it dad" I lean in to him.

"Just do it" I say then lean back up. Mom smiles and kisses his cheek.

"You can do it, and no matter what happens I'm right here. I'll always be here" He's trying to build courage I can tell. He's sweating and clearing his throat. When the words start to come out they're too quiet for anyone but us to hear.

"Here" I say and hand him the microphone. He takes it. Swallows hard then begins.

"Excuse me, Town of Woodland" he's saying while gently tapping on the microphone. Slowly they start to all turn and look his way.

"Towns people. People that I've known my entire life. It seems I have to make a confession to you tonight. A confession of something I done long ago as a silly, rambuntious teenager" He looks my way.

"Go on" I motion. He turns back to the crowd.

"Years ago I done something that I wish I could take back. Boy do I wish. I was out on Halloween night and I drank a little too much. I barely even remember all the details. I honestly wasn't myself"

"Dad, just tell them"

"I gave a young woman a ride. But I didn't take her to where she wanted to go. Instead, I drove to the old barn house and I, I" He stops again, looks down.

"I can't" He says then drops the microphone. He starts to walk away.

"No dad, tell them" I point back towards the microphone and he simply can't resist. His body has to go back and continue. Dad picks up the microphone and continues.

"I did something to her that I shouldn't. I can't take it back but if I could then I would, believe me. I raped this poor girl against her will. She was a good girl and didn't deserve what I had done" The whole crowd is looking in confusion. All to each other. Mumbling among themselves. When one yells out "Is this a joke? Some sort of Halloween prank?"

"Yeah, cause if so, it's not funny"

"It's no joke" I say as I step forward to stand beside my dad.

"My father did just as he has said" Another yells up.

"But why tell us, and now after all these years?" he asks.

"Because, when one does something wrong. One must make it right. And that's what he is doing" "Who cares" comes from the back of the crowd. This tends to spark some mixed emotions from the people.

"Well I think that he's doing the right thing" from a lady dressed as Dorothy from Wizard of Oz.

"I agree"

"Yes, me too"

"Well if he's making it all right then shouldn't he be punished for his crime?" A tall slender man says as he's making his way forward through the crowd.

"Punished?" I say.

"How do you mean, exactly?"

"Well, if it's rape then he should be arrested and maybe have a trial. Let's the towns folk decide his right or wrong" he says.

"No, that simply will not do" I say.

"His punishment is this"

"This?"

"Yes. Your judgement. Your pointing of fingers and name calling. That will be his punishment"

"That's not good enough" one says.

"Yeah. Who was the girl anyhow? What's her name?"

"Give us a name"

"Let her decide his punishment"

"That's impossible" I tell them.

"Why impossible?"

"Because she is no longer with us. She is dead" I say. Shock and sighs go through the crowd.

"So then he killed her too?" comes from one.

"No. That's not my father's crime. He has spoken his. He has done has he needed. Now go, do as you will, but harm him you won't"

"And who's going to stop that from happening?" A voice muffled from the crowd. I just laugh a little then say to them.

"Why I will" I look to the whole crowd and they could feel my power. They felt as if something would happen if they even looked my father's way. I kept my eyes focused on the crowd and made the hanging lights from above them start to blow, one by one.

"Now" I say.

"Let's have a Halloween party" Mom starts to console dad while I walk off the gazebo and towards my new buds. Willow in all her amazement "That was awesome. You must teach me" Everyone goes about the rest of their night. Trying to forget about dads confession and enjoy some of their Halloween. I actually got to see Juliet and Abel. They're not really feeling the new me.

"What's happened to you Gabs?" she says.

"What do you mean?"

"What was all that, and your dad, why would he say those things?"

"Because it's true"

"But why say it, now?"

"He had to make it all right didn't he?" I asked her.

"I'm with Juliet, why would he do it after all these years? And were you making him? Cause it seemed like you were"

"I just simply persuaded him. Now come on, let's go on a hay ride" My Halloween night was turning out to be fantastic. I was finding my true self and I must say, I was loving it. I'm just coming off the hayride and notice Finn leaning up against a tree.

"Proud of you" he says as I turn.

"Hey, I was wondering if I'd get to see you tonight".

"I think things will be alright now" he says.

"I hated that you had to see your old man go through that but I just couldn't rest. When Luella came to me that night to tell me what happened, I was so mad. All I thought of was getting my hands on your father, but her old man took that chance away from me. You've helped and gave me some peace"

"I don't see how"

"It's not what and how I wanted to do it but, this town will punish him. They'll see now that it's not so perfect and that there is wrong here"

"I hate that it was my dad that done this. That brought so much pain to you and Luella"

"It's not your fault. It's not you. Gabby you are, you're different. This town hasn't seen your kind before. I think you will do the town of Woodland some good"

"I'm not sure about that but, I am enjoying the new me. Speaking of that, will it go away now that this has been done?"

"Will what go away? Me and Luella?"

"My powers. Everything that has been happening. I figured it was all you"

"That wasn't me Gabby. That's all been you. You were just ready to receive it"

"Me?"

"You opened yourself up to this"

"But how? I've never heard of anyone in my family like this"

"It's a gift. You have it"

"So, I'm going to keep powers?"

"That's all up to you. If you want them then you'll have them. And if not, then you can probably just let it go"

"No. No. I want them. This could be useful. I mean, I could do good with this. Look at what happened with my dad"

"You can, and you will. But remember, you have to be careful with how far you take it. You can tap into darker things"

"How will I know though?"

"You'll feel it. You can feel when the darkness takes over. It moves in and changes you. All of you. And once it does, it's hard to get rid of it."

This new power that I'm learning I have is wonderful and scary at the same time. I had done a good thing in having my father confess his sins, but how much good really was it? The town hated my parents after that night. My mom had to shut down the diner cause no one would ever step inside since that happened. My father lost his job at the furniture store and has been on the road selling door to door commercial cleaning products. Yeah he done wrong. In fact, they both did since mom knew of that horrible night and did nor said nothing. Was their punishment fitting? I'm not sure, but something had to be done so Finn could move on. And my dad shouldn't have done that. I finished up my senior year and did the whole graduation with my friends. Spent some time with Abel and both shared our future plans. He's wanting to stay here and help his dad with their business while I'm not sure what I'm gonna do. I did apply to a writing school that's just a couple hours from Woodland but I wasn't for sure if I wanted to make that commitment yet or not. I was also trying to spend some time with my little sister Hadley. We spent pretty much our whole summer together. I was seeing sides of my sister that I had never seen before. I even shared with her my new secrets. Showed her some of my new tricks. I was learning to do simple things like change the color of my nail polish or move objects across the room. It was all just fun and games. My parents treated me different since that Halloween night. They seemed to respect me and who I was a lot more. I saw an opportunity one day as I was having a milkshake with Hadley and we were just walking through town. When we came across mom's old diner, and it hit me. We could open it back up but turn it into something different. Maybe a magic shop. That would be something different for Woodland. Like offer some drinks and small snacks and a tarot reading. I was really on cloud nine with this idea. Mom never sold the diner. Only shut it down so she still owned it. I was planning on heading home to talk this over with her. She could use this also. After all, she's been home since Halloween and it's been dad only bringing home the bacon. She could make her specialty desserts and coffee drinks and I'd take care of the rest. Yes, this was definitely on the charts for today. Hadley and I reach home to find mom out back working on her garden and herbs. I ran the idea by her, at first she's not as into it as Hadley and I are, but I think she'll come around. We got the ball rolling on ordering some supplies for our new magic shop and of course some redecorating to transform it into the perfect magic oasis. Took us a few weeks to get it all together and ready for our grand opening. Summer was again coming to an end and Fall was about to be upon us. The perfect time for us to open the shop. The Pixie Dust. The name just came to me and I felt it fitting. We opened on October the first. The year was 1997. I was so excited and ready to explore this new experience and share it with all of Woodland. Hadley had wondered if she would be getting any special powers but I didn't see that happening. She just never seemed to share the interest until now. But I was hoping that I could help her tap into her own natural energies. I had her reading some text books and studying on some things. She was doing good but no real powers yet. So grand opening day. It was a cool, windy day. Perfect for our opening. Hanging banners and signs all over. Made up these cute little trinket boxes filled with bat shaped candles, colored crystals and a few little other specialty items that were magic related. Hadley was handing them out as people entered. Mom was over in her area preparing all the goodies and was also giving out small samples. I was counting on a wonderful grand turnout. Surprisingly people were showing up and showing an interest. Out of all my friends, the only ones that still resided in Woodland were Abel and Chrissy. Well, Chrissy was town over but she stopped by a lot. Everyone else went off to college. Juliet and Ezra got an apartment together in New York since both applied for same school and got in. But she writes me often and calls at least once a week. Chrissy got a job at our local movie rental place. So I do see her quiet a bit. Her cousin Pain and Willow were traveling the world. Willow's grandmother had passed and left her a huge chunk of money so they skipped town and decided to see the world. They send postcards from almost each stop though. Sharing their experiences and saying hi. I was glad that Chrissy and Abel showed up for our opening. They show up with a huge surprise. Oh and, Chrissy and Abel became a couple right after graduation. I think it's great. I love them both and believe they'll be together forever. They really do fit. So they show up, all smiles and could barely hold in their news.

"OK guys, spill" I say to them. They both look at one another.

"What do you mean?" Chrissy says.

"I know something is up. I can tell by that big grin you guys are wearing" She holds up her hand to expose a cute little diamond engagement ring.

"No way, for real?" I say while grabbing her hand to pull it in closer to look.

"That's awesome you guys. Set a date?"

"Not really. I mean I do want it to be a summer wedding and soon, but no actual day has been set in stone yet" As she's still going, Abel motions that he's going to look around inside. She pulls me closer.

"So, what do you really think?" she ask.

"I think it's wonderful"

"Really? You don't think it's too soon do you? We've only known each other about a year and already thinking of marriage. You really think it's great?"

"I do. Now come here. Tell me, what do you think of these?" I say as I hold up my new set of skeleton candles that just arrived. The day was a total success. We didn't sell as much as I would have liked but pretty much the whole town showed up and most seemed to be interested in what we had. Most had never heard nor saw most of the things we had to offer. I do think that our little Pixie Dust has a lot to offer this town.

My 19th birthday was about to be upon us and Hadley had just turned 15. Being so busy with getting the shop ready we didn't really do anything for Hadley's birthday. So I was planning on a big birthday bash at the shop. It would be to celebrate both of our birthdays. And we'd invite everyone, the whole town. Everything was looking good and things seemed to be getting better for mom and dad. Dad got a different job just two towns away at the Electronics Factory. Which meant he was closer to home and would be with us each night now. Mom was enjoying her job at the Magic Shop. She was able to get out and interact with actual people again. While creating all her wonderful desserts. I was loving all the new magic toys that we're coming in. I was learning new things and spells almost every week and was finding out I could do some really amazing things. Ordered all kinds of black and purple balloons, streamers, party hats, party favors and simply just mess makers. I was wanting my lil sis to have the best party ever. Sent out invitations, literally to the whole town.

"Come join us. Help us celebrate two great birthdays all in one day. Have fun. Laugh. Dance. Eat and have your fortune told" I was planning on this party being one that they will always remember. That night finally gets here. Hadley and I are arriving together. Even though I did all the ordering and planning mom wanted to put it all together and surprise us. We arrive, looking all cute of course. As we enter through the front everyone is dancing, laughing and having a good time. They turn to us and yell a loud "Happy Birthday". Each greeting us and saying their personal hello and wishing us the best. The night was really starting off great. And then it happened. I notice a couple of guys that I had never seen before standing over by the food table. They were nice looking. Dressed casual and were grabbing a bite or two. So I ask mom who they were. She didn't know either. Maybe just passing by and decided to stop in the shop? We didn't know but I decided I'd find out. So I approach them. One has red hair and freckles. The other is dark headed.

"Hey" I say. They both turn and look my way.

"How do we know each other?" I ask.

"You friends with my sister Hadley?" The red head answers first.

"Don't believe so" he says then continues shoving finger sized food in his mouth.

"OK. Then do you know anyone else here? Cause I don't know you So it's not me" I ask Finally the dark hair one speaks.

"Chrissy told us about this shop. So we thought we'd check it out"

"Chrissy, oh. That makes sense. So you know Chrissy?"

"Yeah. We've known her all through school. She actually use to date red here" he says as he points to his friend still munching away.

"Cool. Well, my house is your house" I say while I begin to walk away to mingle. I was curious and interested in them. The dark hair boy anyways, but didn't wanna come off as creepy or weird. So I figured I'd move around the crowd a while. Kinda check them out from afar and let them come to me. You know, if interested. I also went straight over to Chrissy so I could get the 411 on these guys. It was so long ago that Chrissy had dated the red head, or Henry. But they've stayed friends. And the dark hair boy, Sebastian Cole, he's been close friends with Henry since forever. Every time you saw one you usually saw the other. Well, I now know his name. It's time to get to know more of Sebastian Cole. Which I plan on doing just that.

Five

I was determined to find out more on this dark haired cutie. Ever since our birthday party and I first laid eyes on Mr. Cole I have been smitten. I couldn't help but constantly talk of him or question I guess you could say, to Chrissy. He wasn't from Woodland so I hadn't got to see him much. In fact, I hadn't saw him since the party. But I was hoping that he would stop by the shop again and soon. It was a Tuesday and I had just opened up and was brewing a fresh pot of coffee. I was the only one in the shop that morning when I heard the chime of the front door opening. I come from the back to see who it was but I didn't see anyone. Odd, I thought. I had looked around a minute but still no sign of anyone. Maybe it was the wind or they changed their mind and left. I went about my business and was opening some new boxes of items that I had just got in. When I heard a small voice from behind me say "Excuse me, Is this on sale?" I turn to see a shorter, middle aged woman standing there holding a piece of fabric.

"Yes, actually it is" I tell her.

"This is the last of this beautiful material that I have left. Sorry it's mis-sized. It's been cut on and I'm afraid this is all I have left" She smiles at me then says "That's OK dear. This is just enough for what I need" I look at her then we turn to walk over to the counter.

"Will that be it then?" I ask.

"Let me see" she says as she lays the fabric on the counter then begins to look around some.

"Take your time" I tell her.

"I'll just be over here opening up new packages. Holler if you need me" She continues to look through the shop while I'm opening up boxes. Then the door opens again. In comes mom and Hadley. They're carrying some fall decor that mom had personally made herself. She places them on the counter. She then turns to Hadley.

"Honey, get the box from the back seat. I forgot about it" she says. Hadley goes on out to retrieve the box.

"Why isn't she in school?" I ask.

"She wasn't feeling well this morning so I let her stay out. Figured she could just come here and help out since she was already up"

"That's actually a really good idea. We just got a new shipment in and she could help unboxing them" With mom and Hadley's arrival I had not paid attention that I had a customer in the store.

"Oh yeah, there's a lady in here" I had told mom.

"What lady?" she asks.

"I don't see anyone"

"She was here just before you guys arrived. See here" I say as I hold up the purple fabric she had placed on the counter.

"She was going to buy this" I look around but I never did see the little woman. I just placed the fabric to the side behind the counter. So if she comes back in I'd have it for her. We went on about our day and around lunch time I did get a visitor. In walked my cute dark haired boy, Sebastian Cole. Finally, I thought. He came in and was looking at some candles. I walk on over. So, any certain color you're looking for?"

"Not sure. Is it suppose to mean something, I mean for different colors?" I just smile.

"Yes. Are you looking to do a spell or maybe rid something from your home?"

"I'm not really looking for anything specific I guess. I'll be honest here. I just wanted to come see you again"

"Me? Well that's a horse of a different color then"

"Horse of a different color?" I smile then say "I'm glad you came in. You don't need an excuse or anything. Just stop by, say hey. I won't mind"

"Well OK" he says.

"Hey. You had lunch yet?" he asked.

"Actually I haven't and I am rather starved" We headed out to grab a burger and left mom in charge a while. We got our lunch to go and sat down by the water near the dam. It was nice to finally get to have a real conversation with him. I hadn't really been interested in anyone since Liam. He was all I thought of for a couple of years, but I'm glad I realized that I deserve better. We were finding out that we had quiet a bit in common. We both love horror movies and both read and collect comics. Both the same age. I enjoyed my lunch date with Sebastian very much. He made sure I got back to the shop and then headed back out. He had to help his buddy move that day. I was excited when I returned and could hardly wait to tell mom and Hadley all about him.

"Mom, he's wonderful. We both like all the same things, and he loves horror just as much as I do"

"That's great Gab. I really hope he works out and I'm glad to see you moving on away from that football player"

"Liam mom, and I agree. Liam never did see me" Hadley comes on over and says "Well his loss. He had his chance and he didn't take it"

"You are right" mom says. We continue on with our day and just before closing I get a customer. It was the little old lady. She startles me. She taps my shoulder just as I'm counting the register.

"Excuse me"

"Oh hey. I never even heard you come in" I say. She smiles at me then motions toward the fabric placed to the side.

"Oh, I laid this to the side for you"

"Yes dear. I'm so sorry that I had to leave in such a hurry last time"

"It's OK. Did you still want it?"

"Yes dear" she says and places a small box of crystals on the counter. "This too"

"Sure" I ring it all up and give her her total. She then pulls out a small sachet with embroidered black thorn and roses on it and counts out her money.

"That's beautiful" I say while admiring it.

"This old thing? It's just something I had lying around and decided to start using it as a change purse. It's the perfect size really"

"Well it's gorgeous" I tell her.

"Thank you dear" she says then takes her items and turns to walk to the door.

"I hope to see you again" I say. She turns ever so slowly my way

"Oh you will dear" then heads on out. There was just something about her. In a way, it's like I knew her. It felt so easy to talk with her. I finished closing up and headed on out. Decided that I would make a stop by the cemetery first. It's been a minute since I had visited there. I hadn't even worked on my book since that Halloween night. Nor had I seen any sign of Finn or Luella. I had assumed that they got their peace since dad told of his wrong doing. I could use the quiet time and planned on just taking a stroll through and maybe sitting a bit by the old oak tree. It was a nice cool night. Kinda cloudy and looked as if it was about to rain some. But the air was so cool and crisp. So refreshing. I didn't have anything to write on, just took some moments of peace and quiet. Things were turning around for my folks since that Halloween. The whole town had pretty much shunned them and made living and walking around in Woodland pure hell. After all, that's why mom closed down the diner and dads been working out of town since. Course they did deserve their punishment. Dad did extremely wrong and so did mom. She knew about it and never said anything. But I was happy that things were getting better for them. Gotta forgive and forget. I had finally moved on with this fantasy I had of me and Liam getting together and found someone, that I was hoping, will be way better for me. After all, everything happens for a reason. It started to get colder, much colder and it seemed darker now then when I had came into the cemetery. I had a light sweater on but it wasn't doing much. Guess I had better head on home. Just as I get up on my feet I noticed a figure or a shadow. Looks as if someone was walking through the graveyard. I tried to just mind my own business and carry on, but I kept seeing like shadows passing by. Then I began to hear whispers. I couldn't quiet make it out, exactly.

"Hello" I said. I know, like a ghost or prowler is going to actually answer back. It was worth a shot though. It took way more than a shadow figure to spook me.

"Is someone there?" more noises of rustling leaves came from behind and were starting to fill the whole graveyard. Figured now would be a good time to try out a new spell I had made up. It was to make something appear or show its self.

"Make known what I hear but cannot see. Make known and appear right in front of me" Just then, I felt an evil that I had never felt before. Darker shadows were approaching but I still could not make them out. I say again.

"Make known what I hear but cannot see. Make known and appear right in front of me" This time a bit more stern. I could tell it wasn't at all happy with me. But it wasn't enough to bring it out. I couldn't get it to show its self. The wind was strong and the night got darker. I stood my ground but it was definitely stronger. It did leave, but it also gave me the creeps. I'll be ready next time. I studied as much as I could and tried out new spells. Made up a few potions that I'd have on hand just in case. Not really knowing what the dark shadow was, I didn't know exactly on what to look up to rid it. As of right now, I would call it the dark shadow. I pretty much left the shop to mom to handle. While I was there but my head was into my books. I had found an old spell book when I was opening up shop one morning. It was in a brown paper bag sitting just outside the door. Thought maybe mom had ordered it but it had no name or address on it. And she knew nothing of it. I took it in and began going through it. It had old writings in it. The pages themselves seemed to be extremely old. Some of the writings were hard to make out. Some appeared to be in the English language but some, I couldn't make out. Was it Latin, Greek? I wasn't for sure. I needed to find someone who could help me read what I couldn't. There were also symbols throughout. Some felt as if I had seen them before. Seemed a bit familiar but I didn't know where, if I had seen them. I spent days and most my nights looking through this book. Trying to figure out as much as I could. I did a little research at our local library and found out some info, but not much.

One evening while I was alone in the shop and sitting at a table we had set up where we usually all sat to have our lunch or just gather a while. The door opened and in walked the little woman who bought the fabric from me.

"Oh hey, it's you" I say to her.

"Yes dear. It seems you could use my help"

"Excuse me?" I ask.

"You have a book you want me to see? So I can help you read it"

"Book? How do you?" She steps forward and places her hand on the book sitting just in front of me.

"This is it, isn't it?" she says.

"Yeah, but how?"

"Never mind that dear. I'll explain all that later. Right now let me see this book" She takes it in her hands. She closes it and then her eyes.

"May I?" she asks as she motions to sit down.

"Oh yes, please" I say to her. She then runs her hands across the cover. Keeping her eyes closed then begins to open it.

"This book dear, it's not simply just a book. In fact, it's not what you would really call a book. It's more of a grimoire. That's been handed down from generation to generation. The hands that have held this. Flipped through its pages have been hands of great nations. May I ask, how did you come by it?"

"I really don't know. You see it was just sitting out by my door one day"

"So you received it as a gift?"

"I guess so" she begins reading some of the inscriptions near the beginning. I couldn't make out the words but she knew what she was reading.

"My dear" she says.

"You have been given a great gift, but use it very carefully. Your talents can take you far but just as far as it can take you, it can also bring you down. Deep down into the lower depths of hell. So deep you will wish that this book never touched your hands" Her words were almost bone chilling. I still wanted to know who had left it on my doorstep.

"So, how did you know I had this?" I ask.

"You came to me in a dream. Well, it's not exactly you, but the image, your face. You appeared to me and I saw a circle around you. Your power how it glowed. I could see so much light and power coming from inside. I followed the light to here that morning"

"So you're a witch too?"

"I never really use that word. Witch is what we are, but honey we are so much more. Once you learn your true potential. Oh the things you will do"

"I have been finding out I can do more. Listen, I came across something in the cemetery last week but it wasn't good"

"Did it try to harm you?"

"I don't think so. It more was just invading my territory. It's like it wanted me to know that it was there"

"What did it feel like?"

"Feel? It felt like death its self"

"I was afraid of that"

"Why do you ask feel instead of look?"

"You will pick up on others energy way before anything else. What did it look like?"

"Just dark shadows. It's like it was one but manifested into multiple. I couldn't get a good image nor could I rid it. It left the cemetery on its own not by my doings"

"Did you try to rid it?"

"I said a little spell I came up with but it didn't work. I could feel it was angering it but it still wasn't enough to make it leave"

We spent hours talking and learning things from the other. It was nice to have someone like me around. Someone I could go to and, who could help me on my journey. She was with me for the rest of the night even as I was closing up shop.

"My name is Gabby by the way" I say as I'm locking the door.

"I know dear"

"Right, you saw me in your dream"

"Only an image in my dream. I saw your name on some papers on the table. Figured it was you. It fit" She says then smiles.

"Matilda Pendle. But it's just Tillie" Tillie would become practically my best friend in the coming days. She was around my parents age. Only about five feet tall, if that. Round happy smiling face. Salt and pepper brown hair. A round pudgy little woman. Sweet as can be. She visited the magic shop almost every day. She was helping me to read the book and also teaching me new spells. The book had inscriptions in it that dated all the way back to 1600. The writing was something Tillie called encryptonic. The spells and teachings in it were each personally written by the witch that had created it. Each had such strong power and were able to grow into their own personal persona. Still not sure of how I received the book but I was determined to learn as much as I could. Even I began installing my own spells and charms into it. Tillie spent many days at the magic shop with me. So much so, she practically became like family. Mom and Hadley even accepted her just as much as I did. My powers became stronger. I was able to pretty much make anything happen that I wanted. Course I was using it all for the good, for now. I had developed a sleep walking power to where I could go into ones dream or mind while they were asleep. A way to get to know them better I guess. To see what they thought of. Things were easy and simple. Another year had passed. Hadley was turning 16 and I 20. My little sis was really becoming a lovely young lady. She was herself too. And I loved that about her. She didn't judge or label others. She accepted everyone into her life and gave them a chance. She got into Cheerleading at school, which I was so happy and proud for her. You see, Hadley didn't fit the typical cheerleading type. She wasn't bubbly headed or judgy. Everyone loved her really. She actually made captain and became pretty popular. She set the standards way different for Woodland High. Her and Emmett had been an item for a while now and they were taking things slow which I was so happy to hear. I myself have been saving myself for the right guy. Been hard at times but I want it to be special and not just another notch in someone's belt. Which leads me back to Sebastian. We've been going out a lot lately and it's getting pretty serious.

Things aren't any easier now that I got my own place either. No parents to help curb those sexual appetites ya know. I share a nice little two bedrooms with Chrissy. Her and Abel still haven't set a date so her and I decided we'd get our own place for the time being. Abel still lives at home and won't live with her until they are married. Which is nice and takes it back old school. I respect that. In fact, things seem to be slowing down for those two. Chrissy says that Abel seems to be different. Like he's pulling away from her. So I figured I'd see what's up with the bestie. Planned a date of pizza and a movie so we could chat. Have some one on one time again and maybe see what's bothering him. Chrissy had to work then was heading over to her parents so we just hung out at my place. Stopped at the local video store first for some classic horror flicks then over to Uncle Gino's Pizzeria for some extra cheese extra pepperoni pizzas. Our favorite. Not my uncle just the name of the best Italian Restaurant in town. The only one in fact. It was nice to unwind and relax for the evening. Felt like we were back in high school again. Him and I spent a lot of nights' side by side. Watching classic horror like Frankenstein, which we both love. And just gossiping about each other's day. Been so Busy with the magic shop and trying to figure out all I could about the book that had been placed on my doorstep. It was nice to catch up with Abel. He and Chrissy had been going out a couple years and spent practically everyday together so I didn't get much alone time with him. We both settled in on the couch. Big comfy blanket, warm fuzzy socks, pizza boxes open on the coffee table and Nosferatu blastin on the screen. All smiles laughing, munching and just enjoying each other's company.

"So Abe, you been good lately?" I ask.

"What do you mean?"

"I don't know. I mean, I don't really see you much. Unless it's coming and going and I just wonder how you are? I mean, Whatcha been up to?" He grabs another slice then settles back in his spot.

"Work. Dads been wanting to open another shop over in George Town so we've just been so busy focusing on that"

"What about you? Your normal everyday life, what about that?"

"What about it?" he ask.

"Chrissy says you've been sorda distant lately"

"I see where this is going" he says as he leans up and pauses the movie.

"You've asked me over so you can grill me about Chrissy. She put you up to this?"

"No. I just wanna know, what's up?"

"It's just complicated with me and her"

"Why? You guys seem so perfect all the time. Why would it be complicated?" I could tell he was growing uneasy with the topic. He began to pace around the room a bit.

"Abe what is it? You can tell me" I assure him while touching his arm. He looks down at my hand. He begins to slowly touch the top but pulls back.

"What's wrong? You know you can tell me anything Abel" He turns away from me then back around.

"No, it's nothing. I've just been so busy lately. So much on my plate. I just feel like I'm neglecting her"

"Is that it? Why don't you tell her how you feel? She'll understand" I did the best I could to be there for Abel and really wanted to see him happy, but I could feel that that wasn't it. Something else was bothering him. And I had planned on finding out just what exactly it was.

Six

It was late by the time Abel and and I finished watching movies so he ended up staying over. In fact, we both fell asleep on the couch. All cuddled up in our warm blanket when Chrissy finally made it back home around 7 am. We wake to her standing there just looking at us. As if we had done something wrong. We both look to one another while wiping the morning away from our eyes.

"Hey" I say to her as she stood motionless. Abel gets on his feet and walks over to her. He kisses her ever so gently on her cheek.

"Good morning" he says while she continues to stand there.

"Chrissy" I say to her "You OK?" She turns to Abel.

"I thought you said you could never stay over. You know, until we got married"

"This?" he says while pointing back to me on the couch.

"This is nothing. This is something Gabs and I have done a million times" I get up and walk over to her.

"Really Chris, Abel and I are definitely no strangers to midnight binging then falling asleep. Happened so many times when we were in school"

"No" she says. "This is different. You guys aren't in school anymore and you" she says while pointing to Abel.

"You said you couldn't stay over until we were married. So why now? Why her and not me?"

"Chrissy you are putting way more into this then you should be. Abel is my best friend. We don't see each other like that, honestly" Just then we both look towards Abel as he stands, looking very confused. Chrissy walks closer to him.

"Is she right Abel?"

"What?" he looks at her with a blank face. I look his way as well.

"Abel, tell her. Tell her we are just friends and that she has nothing to worry about" But he doesn't. In fact, he looks me directly in the face and says "I can't". Chrissy drops her head then runs into her room. Shutting the door behind her. That leaves both of us standing there. Looking, wondering. I'm confused and literally speechless at the moment. He walks over and sits on the couch. Head looking down to his feet. I turn, walk over and sit beside him. There was an awkward silence for, what seemed like forever. Then he takes his hand and places it on my hand which is on my knee.

"I've been feeling feelings for a while now" he says.

"What do you mean, feelings?" I say while both of us continue to look forward. Never to each other.

"I guess I've always known really. I mean, you've always been there. You know everything about me. You're the first thing I think of each morning and the last thing on my mind when I lay down at night" I sat looking forward. Feeling the warmth of his hand on mine. Feeling and even hearing my heart beating inside my chest. I then turn to him. I take his hand in mine and turn his face to mine. I look him in the eyes and words begin to come out.

"I love you more than I have ever loved another human being. Well, besides my family. Abel, you mean so much to me. I could not imagine going through this life not knowing you. I treasure every single moment that we have ever shared. Even the ones where we didn't see eye to eye. You are everything to me and I'm sure you feel the same about me. But, are you sure that it's" Being confused myself and not sure of what to say I pause and try to collect my thoughts and words before they come out. Then I continue.

"Are you sure of what you're feeling? Cause you have a good girl in there" I say as I point down the hall towards Chrissy's room.

"She really is wonderful Abe" He smiles a slight smile then brushes the hair away from my eyes.

"You're right. She is a good girl. Hell I'm lucky to have her. You and I, we're just friends, and I can't mess things up with Chrissy" He gets up, smiles again then heads to her room. At first, she's hesitate to let him in but then she does. They spend hours talking, or at least I guess. I grabbed my keys and headed out. I had to get some fresh air.

To think of what just happened. I mean, at first I wasn't sure what was happening and I was trying to convince Abel and even myself that he wasn't feeling those feelings. He was just being nostalgic. But seeing him walk inside her room and the door shut. My heart ached. What just happened? Did I just do the right thing? I love Abel. I always have but in a friend way. A close friend. And what if we were to cross that line? Would it ruin our life long friendship? I didn't want to ever lose that. Did I even feel that way about him? I mean, he's gorgeous. He's funny and smart. He knows me better than I probably know myself. Was I falling for him? Did I just let what could possibly be the love of my life go? I drove and drove. I had tears rolling down my face. I had never been so confused. I mean, I had Sebastian. He was wonderful. We never argue. He makes me laugh and we have so much in common. Yeah, this is right. Abel has Chrissy. I have Sebastian and we are the bestest friends. So we can't mess any of that up. I'll let him patch things up and I'll just drive. Give them space.

I turned up the radio and hit some back roads. Sang loudly to music that I don't very much care for. By the time I returned to town I had cleared my head somewhat. Headed straight for the magic shop to do some reading. Mom had opened it up since I didn't make it in. It was a quiet day. She was the only one inside. I went in, sat down and began reading while she came from the back.

"I thought I heard the door" she says.

"What happened to you? No one had opened up when I drove by so I came on in. Everything OK?"

"Yeah, just had something I had to do that's all"

"OK" she says then starts to walk away but then turns back.

"Oh yeah, Abel was here looking for you. He says to call him when you can"

"What else? I mean, was he by himself?"

"Nothing else really. And I didn't see anyone. Are you sure you're OK?"

"Yeah, I'm fine. I'll give him a call. Thanks mom" I sat trying to focus on my reading but I couldn't. All I kept seeing was Abel and I laughing. Watching movies. Playing football outside with his dad. His face just stood out in my mind. Now, I guess I was in his place. I wasn't sure what I was feeling and I was so confused. I didn't even know what to say if I called. Do I call? What happened I wonder with him and Chrissy after I left? Just do it. Just call him and get it over with. I sat for a while playing things out in my head. Thinking of what I'd say. My mind was so full of confusion, wonder, hurt. I just didn't know but needed to know. I had to call. It's the only way to find out. Just then I felt a tap on my shoulder. I turn to see, you guessed it, Abel standing there. He has a look on his face. A look of wonder himself, but also kinda like he had to give me news that he really didn't want to.

"Hey" he says. "I came by earlier and your mom said your weren't here. I wanted to make sure everything was OK with us"

"Yeah, she told me. Umm. I just drove. I had something that I needed to do"

"Drove? Where?"

"Just into George Town, nothing really"

"So, everything OK, with us?" he asks.

"Yeah it's fine. Why wouldn't it be?"

"Good" he says with a sigh of relief. "Cause I have something to tell you. Some good news actually, and you're really the only one I wanna tell. At least, before everyone else knows"

"News. OK" I say while he sits down beside me then he says "Chrissy and I have set a date"

"A date? Oh wow. That date"

"Yeah. You were right. She's wonderful and I almost screwed that up. Thankfully we fixed it"

"Yeah. She is great. I love her like a sister. And you, well I've always loved you and you know that. I want you to be happy Abel"

"I know, and I didn't mean to say those things earlier. I, I don't know what I was doing. Guess I was just getting cold feet about the engagement. But you don't have to worry. I'll not cross those bounds again" he says then stands to his feet. Gives me a hug then tells me he needed to be going cause Chrissy was out in the car waiting and that they were heading to Weaver for a romantic outing. Weaver is a small town about two hours away where mostly everyone goes to get away. That is, if you're looking for something exciting and new, then you head to Weaver. So that's that. I watched this man walk out the front door and into the beginning of the rest of his life.

The next two days were actually pretty painful. I carried on like normal. Opened the shop. Closed the shop. But all I thought of was Abel and Chrissy. What were they doing that very moment? I kept busy at work so I had an excuse to distance myself from Sebastian. I really didn't know how I now felt about him and where things stood with us. I focused on my books and even did some meditation just to see if it would help at all. Done a couple of simple spells. Hoping to take my mind off Abel and Chrissy. I came across an old ancient lover's spell. I stared at the page a while. The words went through my mind, but I didn't want anything fake. I didn't want to harm either of them, and I knew that what Abel and I already had was far better than any spell could create. No, I slammed the book shut. If it's meant to be then it will be. I'll just dig myself deeper into my reading and learning more of this encryptonic language. I hadn't seen much of Tillie lately so I figured I'd go check on her. Maybe she'd have some advice on my love trainwreck. As I reach her doorstep I could see a gathering of women. A small crowd dressed in long garments, old antique jewelry and looked kinda like gypsies in a way. I step up on her front porch and they all drop down like they are bowing to me. One looks my way but stays on the ground. She holds out her hand and says "If I may?"

"Yes of course" I say to her

"Get up"

"No" she says while motioning for the others to stay down.

"You are the chosen" she says then looks back towards the ground.

"Chosen? You must have me mistaken for someone else. Please, get up, all of you" But they do not. The spoken one continues.

"You are her. We can feel you. Your power is beautiful"

"Who is her though?" I ask.

"She is the one who can open up our eyes. She will lead us from here. She is the one with the power from our ancestors. She is you" Just then Tillie opens the door.

"Come in child. Never mind these fools" She takes me by the hand and gently pulls me through the small crowd. Shuts the door behind us.

"Sit" she says as she motions towards the sofa.

"Tillie, what is all that? Who are those women?"

"They are old century charmers"

"What's that exactly? And what did they mean by, I am the one?"

"They come from a line of witches but most do not have any special powers. They can foresee things and feel things, but that's about it. They live their life in search of this special witch. With powers to create a new world for witches. One in which we are not condemned nor hated. They believed that it was I at first, but I think they were feeling something else. Someone else, close by" "But who, if not you?" I simply ask. She looks at me with such straight face and says "You dear".

"That can't be. I mean, I don't come from any line of witches and I'm just learning all this myself. Why would they think me?"

"They feel dear. A Charmer's feelings are usually never wrong. They were mistaken when they found my doorstep. They were merely feeling you through me. Now that you have came here and they seen you in person. They'll know for sure who the real enchantress is" She says then hands me a locket.

"Open it" Inside is a picture of one of the most beautiful women I had ever seen in my life. Long dark curly hair. Dressed in a beautiful neck collar dress. A rose hairpin gently pulling back the sides. And a lovely spider broach on her chest.

"She's lovely. Who is she?" Tillie leans in closer to me.

"Look closely dear. Don't you feel it?" I'm looking at her face and feeling like I'm transported back in time for a moment. I see a lovely lady sitting in a tall back chair sewing what looks to be a blanket. Sitting by the fire in a large beautiful home. Quietly humming a melody. It seems familiar. Like I've heard it before. She's sitting there as a man comes into the room. He's telling her to get up. She stands to her feet. I can see she's pregnant. She's pulling away from him but he's trying to get her to do something. To follow him. He's trying to lead her into a small hideaway in the wall. But she shakes her head no. He grabs her, pulls her closer and kisses her. She places her head on his chest. Just then the door is rushed open and a crowd comes inside. They pull them apart and take the woman. The man fights but then a gun is pulled and takes his life. The woman screams. All the crowd ducks down. The windows are blown out by her scream. Everyone spaces themself from the woman. She falls to the floor to embrace the man. He is gone. There is no more breath inside. The beautiful woman stands to her feet. Her eyes turn black as night. Hair flows but there's no wind. She turns toward the towns people. Raises her arms and opens her mouth. Black birds come from inside and fill the room. The curtains begin to burn. The flames were everywhere and no one can escape. All who are inside perish. Except for the beautiful woman. She walks through the inferno unharmed. Then suddenly I'm back to reality.

"Tillie, what did I just see?" she smiles.

"She is Lady Catherine Vonness"

"Who is that?"

"Lady Catherine was your great great grandmother"

"But how? My mother never mentioned anyone like this"

"No, she wouldn't have, especially since she never knew her"

"How do you know about her?"

"Lady Catherine is a wonderful beautiful person"

"Why do you keep saying is? Don't you mean was?"

"Oh no dear. Lady Catherine is very much alive"

"But how? That would make her almost 200 years old"

"An encrypt witch never dies. Their body may not be with us, but their spirit very much is"

"I want to meet her"

"You have much to learn my child, but much will be rewarded"

"So tell me more about my great great grandmother. How is it you know of her but my parents don't?"

"You see, after most of the towns people perished in the fire that night and Lady Catherine lost the love of her life, she put a curse on Woodland. A curse that would bring so much hatred and evil. Sadness would fall upon this little town. She herself left and headed as far away as she could. But only after she had her baby girl whom she named

Abigail Rose. She left Abigail with a poor farmer and his wife. She couldn't bare to look upon her sweet baby's face and not see her beloved. She thought she'd be better off with a normal family. Hoping that she wouldn't have to go through the suffering and ridicule that she herself had endeared over the years. Lady Catherine went on with her life as far away from Woodland Grove as she could. Her baby Abigail Rose grew up not knowing of her true mother nor her powers. If one is not taught before a certain age the power usually fades. So your mother, her mother and her mother lived normal everyday lives. Not knowing of their true powers".

"Wait, Are you telling me that I come from a long line of actual witches? Even my mom?"

"That's what I'm saying"

"Then how am I the only one to feel anything? To do anything, magical?"

"Because you felt it. You accepted it before it was too late. Your mom, grandmother and great grandmother, they did not"

"Accepted what really?"

"You let it in. When you sat in that graveyard and wrote those words onto paper. You accepted it."

"But what about mom and Hadley? Hadley's still young. Can't see accept it?"

"She would have showed signs by now."

"So, those women outside, what am I to them? Am I like their leader or something?"

"Something like that dear." Tillie says then hands me a small black sachet.

"Here. I have been waiting many years to be able to hand this over to its proper owner." I take it and slowly began to open it. It's a soft velvet material with a small embroidered black rose on it.

"Hey" I say.

"It's like the one you have." She smiles at me and nods yes. I continue to open it. Inside is a beautiful black spider broach and a note. The broach was identical to the one Lady Catherine, I mean my great great grandmother had on. I open the note. It had the same writing as the grimoire that I had received at the shop. The writing was encryptonic English language. A writing used only by witches. Guess it was to keep others from knowing their secrets. Tillie smiled at me.

"It's yours dear. The broach has found its way home. Take the note and keep it close by. In time you will understand its writing and you will then know what Lady Catherine wants to tell you"

"But how am I going to learn how to read the language?"

"You will as you get stronger and study from the book more. You will understand and be able to read its language. It's sacred and not for everyone. That's why it's not as easy just to pick up and read."

Seven

I spent many nights reading and trying to understand the witches grimoire. A little each day the words would come to me. I started seeing the writing like it was regular English. I started working on the spells and chants and felt my power growing. I could change day into night and Monday into a Friday if I wanted. I held so much power into my hands. Which got me thinking of what Tillie had said about Woodland. Catherine had placed a curse on the town before she left. A curse to bring pain and suffering. But why place the curse then leave her newborn baby in the same town? Maybe that's why our little town had so many tragic events to happen but then they would go on like nothing happened. Maybe they were programmed to carry on. Maybe I could stop this curse. After all, it was my bloodline that caused it. Tillie also said that Catherine's spirit is very much with us. Could I bring her back somehow? I'd have to check the book for this one. Things with me and Sebastian were getting really weird. Guess it was more me. I just didn't want to be with him anymore. I pulled away more and more each day. Not really wanting to actually break up I guess. I tried to focus on my learnings and not on what Abel and Chrissy were doing. But it really didn't help.

After Abel let it out how he felt that day I just couldn't forget it. It was tearing me up to see him with Chrissy and it was getting harder for me to hide it. Like if they were to show affection to one another around me then things would happen. Things like lightbulbs blowing if they kissed or stuff falling off a shelf. It was beginning to get a little darker. Just the other day they stopped by the shop and as they sat here talking with me, Chrissy reached over and grabbed Abel's hand. I felt as if my blood was boiling inside. I felt more anger this time. As if he was mine and she was crossing lines that she shouldn't. Chrissy then begin to choke. It was like she couldn't breath or something was caught in her throat. Abel tried to help her and started to panic a little. While I remained calm and focused on her. My eyes never blinked and Abel said it looked like they turned black as coal. But once I blinked it's like it stopped. Chrissy started breathing normal. She then ran out crying while Abel just looked at me. It's like he knew this time. He got up from his seat but before he left. He turns to me and says "We need to talk. I'll be back later" then he heads on out. Guess the cat was out of the bag.

My feelings for Abel were definitely much more than a friendship zone. And it was getting obvious to others too. I went about my day not caring that I had almost choked my friend to death. After all, she had something that didn't belong to her and I was about to change that. I did a cleansing of the shop hoping to release any negativity and hate. I mean, I didn't want to harm anyone. I just wanted what I wanted and my feelings for Abel were becoming so much stronger especially since I wasn't able to spend much time with him lately since everything came out that day. Before Abel got back to the shop I had another visitor, Sebastian. I could tell he wanted to talk as he entered. I could feel his energy. He was so lost and confused with us lately.

"Hey" he says while approaching me.

"Hey" We both exchange our awkward heys then he sits at the table. I walk on over and sit across from him.

"Where's this going Gabby?" he asks.

"I really don't know. I mean, I never wanted to hurt you. And I didn't know that it would turn out like this."

"Yeah it's pretty shitty"

"I'm sorry Sebastian. I enjoyed everyday we had together, I did. But things have changed within this last year. I've changed"

"I've noticed. Why can't you just talk to me Gabs? We started out so close at the beginning. What happened? And don't say it's about that stupid book or your powers. I've gotten use to it. I accept who you are. I've never tried to stop you or change you in any way. Why can't you just let me in?"

"I don't love you Sebastian. I mean, I adore you so much. But I just do not love you. And that's not what you want or deserve. You deserve someone who truly loves you, and I'm sorry but it's not me" We both sat there in silence a bit then in walks Abel. Talk about perfect timing. Sebastian turns to him then back to me, then says as he is getting up.

"I think I know why"

"Why what?" I ask.

"Why you can't and won't love me. You can't when you're already in love with someone else" he says then leaves. Abel looks my way "What's that about?"

"We just had a long overdue conversation that's all. Anyhow, you wanted to talk?"

"Yeah, this thing with you and Chrissy has to stop"

"I don't know what you're talking about"

"You know. I saw you today. Earlier, your eyes Gab, they were black as coal. And I've noticed that weird things keep happening when we're together. That was no accident with Chrissy today, and she knows too"

"You're just imagining things Abe. I wouldn't harm either of you"

"Wouldn't you? But what I can't figure out is why. Did she do something to make you angry?"

"Really, I'm not doing anything. You're just being paranoid"

"I don't think so. You just need to stop before someone really gets hurt Gabby"

"Enough about that. Let's talk about what we're going to do this Halloween for the big bash"

"You can't just change the subject and think that it will make it go away. I mean it Gabby. I want it to stop" I could tell that Abel was pretty upset over this one but it also just fueled my anger as well. I wasn't mad at Abel, only Chrissy. And it made things worse that I lived with her. Although I had been spending most of my nights back at mom and dads I did still reside back at the house with Chrissy. I figured I would move out before my anger did get the best of me. I honestly didn't want to harm her but my love for Abel was growing stronger.

I did just that, moved out and back home with mom, dad and Hadley. I missed our time together anyhow. So moving back was a pretty good decision. It helped me take some time away from Chrissy and Abel. Hopefully it would help calm things. Halloween night rolled around and everyone was planning on being at the big Halloween bash in town. For us at the magic shop we had it all decked out. Had a bunch of freebies we were giving out as well. Saw Sebastian with a new lady friend and I can honestly say that it didn't bother me one bit. I was actually happy for him. Chrissy had made an appearance at the shop before everyone started showing up. I had a few customers inside the shop at the time when she entered. She walked around a while as if she was looking for something. But I knew she wanted to talk. After I rang up the last person I walked on over to her.

"Hey, looking for something?" I asked. She turns to me.

"Actually, not really. I just wanted to talk. I miss us. What has happened?" Now I could just come out and tell her that I was in love with her finace or I could just keep it inside and go on like it was before my head and heart decided it wanted Abel more than a good buddy.

"I think I've just been so busy with work lately and this thing with Sebastian, but I think it's all pretty much over now" I say to her. Decided to go with a lie. After all, if I admit my true feelings then things will just be worse. So, a lie it is.

"Good. Cause I'm gonna need you for my upcoming wedding. So many plans and things to do. Plus I want you to be my maid of honor"

"Wow. That's a pretty big honor. Are you sure you want it to be me? I mean, what about WIllow?"

"I'm not even sure if they'll make it. You know them. In fact, I'm not even sure where they are right now"

"Right. Well then, you guys are in no hurry though right? I mean a date hasn't been set in stone yet"

"Didn't Abel tell you? It'll be a Spring wedding. The first of April"
"That soon?"

"Yeah I know, but I've already got some ideas and it'll be just a small gathering" OK so, now I was on a time crunch. I had to break up this wedding before April. Normally I'm not the mean spirited one who tried to destroy her best friends life but this was different. I really felt like Abel and I belong together, and it was time to find out. The Halloween bash was going great. Just like it always does. I played nice with all my guest, including Chrissy. If I were to be with Abel then I want it to be right. I don't want it forced or anything. I know he already had some feelings for me. Feelings other than friendship. But I wanted it to come from him and be true. I wanted no magic to be a part of our love. I'm handing out refreshments when a younger lady approaches. She's dressed in an 1800's type dress. Smelled of Lavendar. As she comes to me, a broach on her chest catches my eye.

"That's lovely" I say to her as I hand over a small cup of cider.

"Why this?" she says while placing one hand over it.

"It was my mothers"

"Well I think it's gorgeous. In fact, I have one something like it" I say as I reach in a small satchet placed just under the counter, and take out my own to show her. I'm holding it in my hand over the counter when she leans in for a closer look.

"That is beautiful. The markings are so similiar to mine" We both spend some time admiring one anothers broach then Tillie comes up to us.

"Tillie look" I say to her.

"Her broach is so much like mine" Tillie leans in for a closer look.

"So it is" she says then looks to the girl.

"Would you mind leaving us for a moment dear?" The young lady smiles and nods then turns to walk away.

"Is something wrong?" I ask Tillie.

"Oh no dear, but you must be careful who you show your broach to"

"Why's that?"

"That broach is no ordinary broach. It's not just a piece of jewelry you would find in a typical store child. It's magical and it needs to be kept up. In good hands and away from others"

"She seemed so harmless though. Just a girl in a costume. What's it gonna hurt?" Then suddenly, just as the words left my mouth. A gust of wind came across the room. It grew dark and cold. No others were there with us, even though there was just a crowd of people. It was just Tillie and I. Standing across from us was the young lady with the broach.

She stood, dark eyes, hair flowing and holding her arms out, she began to chant a spell of some sort. Then Tillie throws back her arm and says beounto. Which throws me back out of the way. So it's just the two of them. They both focus their attention and power on the other and each throwing a hand up and saying spells. They begin fighting back and forth then finally the young woman yells "ENOUGH...This is not your fight Matilda: She knew Tillie by name but who was she?

"You will not harm this child"

"Child? She is no child. You've seen the prophecy. You know what she will do. Who she will become"

"I've seen a foolish old mans ramblings. A man who has already lost his mindset"

"Who has told of many happenings already. Things that have definitely came true"

"Gabriella is not the person in those dreams. She comes from a different family and knows no harm. She is good Mordilla. Now be gone"

"Very well. But when, and I do say when, the time comes that any of the events that have been foretold start to happen. Then I will, along with many others, will return to handle it" She says then looks my way.

"Keep hold of that broach dear. It's the only thing that will save you" then turns and leaves the shop. Everything goes back to normal. Music playing, crowds gathering.

"Tillie. What was that?"

"I was afraid of this" "Of what exactly, and what is this prophecy about me being evil?"

"It's nonsense child. A foolish old warlock named Artemis who thought he could see the future"

"Well can he? I mean, am I evil? Will I become evil?"

"No deary. You have too good of a heart" But did I? I was already plotting to break up Chrissy's wedding, and what about the day she almost choked to death? Maybe the old warlock was right.

"What did he see exactly Tillie?" But she refused to answer. Just stood there drinking her drink.

"Tillie....I need to know. What was it?"

"Go enjoy your party dear. This is no night for any of this. After all, it's Halloween. It's our night dear. A witch's night" I couldn't get Tillie to give me any straight answers but I wasn't going to forget it. I'd let it go for the night but first thing tomorrow, I'll be looking for this warlock Artemis. I carried on with my party and even walked around town a while.

Enjoyed my evening and thought nothing else of Mordilla or this old warlock Artemis, at least not until I saw the woman again. This time, standing by the big tree near the gazebo. She wasn't alone. There were three other women dressed in the same 1800's clothing. All standing there in a circle holding hands. I get closer and see a naked lady with long red hair sitting in the center of them. She's holding a bunny in one hand and in the other an ancient looking knife. They start swaying back and forth while chanting something. I can't quiet make it out, for they are too quiet. Then the naked lady pierces the bunny with the knife and lets the blood drip all over her. I look around to see if others are seeing this but no one acts as if they do. Then the same one from earlier, Mordilla, turns to me. She then starts pointing my way. Opens her mouth and all I could feel was cold and darkness. Tons of bats were flying out and straight towards me. I duck down and cover my head with my arms til they passed. When I looked up Mordilla is standing right in my face. I jumped back. She moves forward in such speed then screams just loud nothingness. I close my eyes and say a small spell for her to be gone. When I slowly open my eyes she is no longer there. None of them are. I immediately head back to the shop to see Tillie about this. I could barely get the words out.

"Calm down child" she says "You look as if you've seen a ghost"

"I'm not sure what I saw. I know one was the lady from earlier, but then there was more with her. They were chanting, swaying and blood. There was blood dripping all over the naked lady. And that poor bunny. Then she was right in my face. Oh Tillie, her face was so dark. I could feel all their darkness. This Mordilla is not good at all"

"No dear. Mordilla was one of the darkest, coldest, most evil of all us witches. She wanted to be the most powerful and did not want to accept her simple powers. She tapped into things that no one should ever call upon"

"And she says I'm the evil one?"

"Mordilla is a lost witch. And being that is not a good thing at all. Once she called upon the darkest of our magic and found out she couldn't handle it, she has been wandering since"

"The darkest?"

"Yes dear. It's so dark that we must not even mention its name. For its name alone can do so much" She says then takes out a pen and begins to write something on paper. She hands it over to me but before releasing it from her grip, she says "Only read it once. And never say it out loud" she then releases it to me. I look down at it and see the name Azrul. After reading it she grabs the paper from my hand and burns it.

"Never speak of him"

"Him? it's a person?"

"Yes. A very dangerous dark demon"

"Then why did Mordilla call upon him?"

"She wanted more power. Power that she had was never enough for her. She found an old spell book and began experimenting with it. She tried to make up her own and create things that were simply impossible, but nothing ever worked. Or at least was never enough to please her. Then one summer night during a full moon. She had done the unthinkable. She brought her young sister of only 12 years to the great mountain. Placed her on a rock. Bound her wrist and ankles so she could not run away. She then sacrificed her only sister to a higher power. To anything that would give her more. This called out one of our worst enemies. A dark demon who feeds off of a witches power. Mordilla only got darker and grew away from her heritage. She became more like the demon, always doing his dirty work. We tried to save her but nothing ever could break that hold that he had on her"

"But I don't understand. Why is she after me if she thinks I'm going too become evil?"

"It's your power dear. Mordilla is simply afraid that you will be stronger than her"

"Why and how?"

"She feels it. Just like you can feel others energy and if they are evil or not. We all feel your power"

"Why didn't I feel anything from her the first time?"

"She placed a simple spell that would hide her true identity. That's why I couldn't tell who she was at first. But I sensed something was off. After I asked her to leave it helped clear my mind and I then saw Mordilla."

Each day I was growing stronger in my powers and learning more of where I came from. And each day I was getting closer to finding a way to bring Lady Catherine back.

Eight

My mission was to find out how to bring Catherine here in the present, and then I'd turn some focus over to making Abel realize that it is us that are meant to be wedding in the near future. I had done some studying on the ancient witches of Woodland Grove and found some wonderful facts on the Vonness family. This was, after all, my family and bloodline. I wanted to dig deeper into this and find out what I could. My great great grandmother made a decision in which she thought was the best for her and her baby at the time. I wanted to find my great great grandmother. To actually speak to her in person. The grimoire held many wonderful ancient spells. Spells to call upon the dead. To bring them back upon Earth. But according to Tillie, Catherine was not dead. She was merely a spirit without a body. So, I think I have found the perfect spell.

The night came that I was finally ready to begin my spell. To call out Catherine from whence she resides. I placed eight black candles around my person. Lined a circle around me made of clover. Removed all earthly garments for purity and cleared my mind of all. I recited the spell several times while each time lighting a black candle. Over here through space and time I call upon thee bloodline of mine. Catherine Vonness do hear my plea. Come to me now of spirit be. Each time I felt the air get duller. The room was darker and became much colder. I repeated myself over and over, but I felt no presence. No Catherine.

I was about to give up when suddenly a burst of wind crossed my shoulder. Someone or something was with me. I sat in silence for a moment. Only hearing my breathing and my own heart beating. Then a dark shadow appeared before me. Not sure if it was evil or good. I played it slow. I waited for it to make a move. It sorda hovered just outside my circle. It was as if it couldn't enter.

"What are you?" I say. It continues to sit there in silence then after a few seconds, it starts to dart around the room.

"Catherine. Grandmother?" I ask. It continues to move about the room. Then a thought occured to me.

"Azrul?" I ask. Could it be the demon of darkness? The wind began to get stronger. There was a strange odor filling the air. This has to be something of evil. It can't be Catherine. So I sturdied myself and made my voice deeper and without fear.

"Azrul. It is you, isn't it?" I asked for the final time. Then the dark shadow started to take shape. It began to form into a very handsome man. He looked kind with gentle eyes and a frail face. Had on garments from looked to be from the 1800's. It formed solid then just stood there. No words or motion. Just silence.

"Hello" I say to it. "Do you have a name?" It still stayed motionless. With only a tilt of his head. "I am Gabby" He smiles then begins to mumble my name.

"Gabby?"

"Yes. Gabriella Delaney actually. And what is your name?"

"My name" he says while looking very puzzled.

"Yes. You do have a name don't you? What do people call you?" He takes a moment. Looking around a bit then back to me.

"They call me Azrul"

"But that can't be. You are, I mean, I'm told you are evil. In fact, one of the most evil demons ever to grace the Earth" He looks in amazement. Then places his hand over his chest.

"Me? I am evil?"

"Yes. So they say"

"They must be mistaken. I only came because you called me. I come to help. I am not evil, nor am I a demon"

"I didn't call you. I was looking for my great great grandmother"

"Yes. Lady Catherine" he says then holds his head high with eyes closed.

"Lady Vonness holds dear to my heart. You say she is your grandmother?"

"Great Great, but yes she is"

"Lady Catherine is great to all of us"

"So you know her?"

"I know her well my child"

"Then you know where she is or how I can get in contact with her?"

"Why yes, she is with us all"

"What do you mean?"

"Lady Catherine lives and walks amongst us all daily. Why do you ask this?"

"I need to talk to her. Can you bring her here?"

"She is already here child. Just look around. Speak from your heart. She will hear you"

"I don't understand" Just then a warmth came across me. It was as if I'm receiving a hug from a loved one. A tiny voice called out as it passed.

"Don't speak to him. Say no more. He is evil" It was like someone was trying to warn me. Was it Catherine? Was this the true demon Azrul? I immediately blew out one candle. Hoping to break the connection and Azrul would leave. It did just that. I blew out the first one then the second until they were all out. Did I just call upon and bring forth the evil demon Azrul? And was my great great grandmother trying to help? My powers were growing stronger each and every day. But I was even more determined to find Catherine and bring her back now more than ever. I consulted with Tillie the next day about my findings. I felt sure that it was my great great grandmother trying to warn me of the demon Azrul. I felt a comfort and warmth in knowing that Catherine was around us, in a sense. I wanted to bring her forth, in a body form. If I'm this great high witch they all speak of, then I should be able too. Tillie had dug out some ancient spells that were handed down to her from all the great witches before. She thought between her and I, that we could find or create a spell to bring back Catherine. We worked day and night. Reading and even brewing up our own potions. Anything that would give us our Lady Catherine back. Each with no luck. I could feel us getting closer though.

One evening as Tillie and I sat in the cemetery and read out a few spells we got as close as to bringing forth Catherine in a spirit form. She was lovely. Just like when I saw her before when Tillie first handed me the locket. She appeared to us wearing a beautiful Ivory colored neck collar dress. Long brown hair flowing with gentle curls. We both stood waiting for her to speak first.

"My great great granddaughter Gabriella. It is so nice to see you in person" I just smile to her as I look upon her smiling warm face.

"You look so much like my baby girl Abigail Rose. I have watched you all for years. Making sure you were safe" she says. And inside, I've always felt like someone was with me, watching over.

"Lady Catherine, Grandmother. We need your help"

"Yes my dear, anything"

"We want to bring you back. To give you a body, but we can't seem to find the right spell"

"And you won't dear. We come from a very powerful line of witches, but once our earthly bodies die. They can never be brought back"

"That's before. I want to change that. I, we" I say while motioning to Tillie.

"We want to give you an earthly body. And we've gotten really close but, something keeps stopping us. I mean, it's like we're right there but then it just slips away. That's where you come in. Maybe you can help with the spell and we can actually pull it off"

"I don't see that there's anything I can do, but I don't mind trying" Both Tillie and I were elated to hear her say this. We again set out to creating the perfect spell to bring our Catherine back. We could speak with her occasionally, but it would drain us all afterwards. So, we were limited on our times that we got to talk one on one with Catherine. So many things were happening lately. Everyone was going on with their lives while I spent most my days working on potions and spells. I didn't see much of Abel and Chrissy and it was getting closer to their wedding day. I had to find some time to making him realize that I'm the right one. I planned an evening out with just him and I. At first, Chrissy didn't want him to go after what happened at our last movie night, but Abel convinced her that I'll always be in his life so she'll have to get use to it. He also reassured her that she had nothing to worry about. It wasn't anything fancy. Just planned on a burger and shake from the old drive in, like old times. Then either a movie or just a drive around town so we could catch up. It was all going really well actually. We laughed so much while getting a bite to eat. Not letting all the other little things that's been happening bother us. It was like we were back in high school.

Afterwards, we decided to drive out by the dam to just sit and talk. I wanted for our love to be real. For what both of us felt for the other to be genuine. Nothing from a spell or forced. So I never did any, but I did say a small chant for him to be honest. He would speak from his heart. He wouldn't be able to hide or anything. I began by asking him if he was sure that marrying Chrissy was the right thing. At first, he just sat there. Looking out the front window. Then he drops his head.

"Tell me Abel, Is this really what you want?" He then turns towards me.

"No" then drops his head again, but only for a second. Then he immediately looks back at me and places his hand on my cheek. We both look at one another then he moves closer in, and it finally happens. He kisses me. It was deep, passionate and warm. It was so nice and so long waited. He pulls back, then says to me.

"I'm sorry Gabby. I really must be confusing you, but I can't keep hiding it"

"It's OK Abel. I feel the same way"

"It's weird though. I mean, I love Chrissy, I do, but I'm not sure if I'm in love with, her. I think I'm in love with you" I smile, inside and out. I've waited for this for so long. But I didn't want it to be fake. So I refused to do any spells to speed up or hinder the process. He then turns to me.

"Are you sure that you're not doing this?"

"What do you mean?"

"You didn't put some kind of love spell on me did you?"

"No, honestly Abel, this is all you. It's real"

"It doesn't matter. Cause I know what I want now. And it's you" We spent some time making out in the front seat of Abel's car then realized that we had to get back to reality and tell others about this. Others, like Chrissy. We both care so much for her, but it would be unfair for us all if we continued on like we were. We both figured it would be better if Abel tells Chrissy by himself. So, I head over to the magic shop and decide I'll wait for him there. He continues on home to find Chrissy waiting on his arrival. He walks in and just stands there a moment. Trying to build up the courage and find the right words to say. She notices him there.

"Oh hey" she says then pats the couch beside her.

"Come sit down. You can finish this movie with me" He takes a moment then moves on over to the couch.

"So how was your night?" she asks.

"That's actually what I wanted to talk with you about" She mutes the TV then turns to him.

"OK. What's up? Let me guess, she doesn't wanna be in the wedding? I kinda figured this was gonna happen"

"Well I guess you could say that"

"I knew she would flake on us"

"She's not going to be in the wedding cause there isn't going to be one"

"Wait, what?"

"This is hard enough so I'm just gonna say it" But before he could get the words out. She jumps off the couch and begins to pace about the room. Crying and rambling on, things like. I knew it. She did this to you. You guys have both been acting weird lately. Abel grabs her by the shoulders.

"Stop" he says.

"This isn't her fault. If anyones it's mine" He turns away but they both stand in silence a while.

"I've always loved her really. I tried telling you both but you wouldn't listen. But it can't continue like this. We all owe it to one another to find out where it's gonna go. It wouldn't be right or fair if you and I married and we weren't meant to be. Now is the time that we figure this out" That was pretty much it then he left Chrissy to take it all in. He was right. We all needed to see where this was going. Especially before they wed and it ended up being a mistake.

I waited at the shop with mom and Hadley. I somewhat filled them in on what had happened but even I wasn't for sure on what exactly we were going to do now. I also wasn't for sure if Abel was going to return or not. After all, it couldn't be easy telling your fiancée that you no longer wish to marry them. I wouldn't want to be in his shoes. But he did return, and surprisingly he looked somewhat happy.

"Well I guess we'll leave the two of you to talk" mom says while her and Hadley head out for the evening.

"I'll lock the door behind us so you'll get no interruptions dear" she says. Leaving Abel and I to ourselves.

"So" I say to an ever so handsome Abel standing across from me.

"So" we both kind of smile and stand there.

"How did it go with Chrissy?"

"She's not too happy"

"I'd say not"

"But like I told her. This has to be done. You and I need to see where this is going with us. And what better time, before the wedding"

"I agree"

"I mean, I don't want it to hurt our friendship. If things don't work out. You mean so much to me Gabs"

"It won't. We have too much in this. Not many have a friendship like we do. No matter what happens I'd say we'll always be friends"

"I hope you're right" We took some time over the next few days to really talk and just spend quality time together. It was nice to take my mind off all this evil with Azrul and trying so hard to bring Catherine back. Still shocked that we were both fixing to turn 20 and we're both still virgins. He comes from a very religious family and holds firm to the no sex til marriage and I just haven't found the right one. Sure I was highly attracted to Sebastian and we came close many times but I also wanted to wait until marriage. Sometimes I feel it was fate. That Abel and I were truly meant to be together so our subconscious minds simply wouldn't allow us to give our bodies to anyone else. At least, that's what I'd like to believe. I think we made the right decision on being together. It all felt so right. We both already loved each other so very much. Now it was maturing into a real romance.

Months went by and summer flew by quick. It was fall once again and I had been neglecting my time with Tillie and finding a spell to bringing Catherine back. But I explained to Abel who she was and how much it meant to me to bringing her back here in the present. That I needed to get back into my studying and finding the right spell. He of course totally understood. Tillie caught me up on her new findings. She had found an ancient spell. One in which you must be extra careful when doing it so you don't release yet another demon. The Baltar demon: A demon who can be helpful if used correctly, but one must never trick or misuse this demon. For his wrath can be very harmful and even deadly. We got everything ready and began placing our 8 black candles around us. We held hands and said a small protection spell before starting the true spell. Tillie sprinkled some shadow dust. A potion created by witches to trap a demon or spirit in its shadow form so it can't hurt you. We both then began the spell. Spirit of deep, your soul it wanders. Find your way here, you will surely not squander. Come to us Catherine. Come to us Spirit of deep. Come to us. We say this several times and surely enough Catherine appears. Her image is faint. Kinda blurry and see through but then it starts to get stronger and become more solid. We say it once more as the wind begins to blow. There's a darkness and that same odor as before.

"She's appearing. It's working" I say to Tillie.

"Yes child. But do not let go of my hand and never leave the circle" she says. We say it once more. Catherine is there. She's happy. She's smiling, but then there's this dark shadow that moves through the room. The wind is picking up. It's howling. Tillie is gripping me tighter.

"I don't like this child" she says as we both stand our ground.

"Catherine, you must say it with us. Maybe your power with ours will do it" I say. She tries. We all 3 begin repeating the spell once more but the shadow is becoming more angry. Tillie releases her grip from my hand. She reaches down and picks up a small black locket hanging from an old rusted chain. She holds it up and begins to chant something. It was hard to make out with all the wind and it sounded like it wasn't in English. She chants it several times and finally the shadow leaves but as it does it goes straight through Catherine taking her with it.

"NO" I yell out. I then run towards her trying to grab her hand. But it was too late. They were gone. I turn to Tillie.

"We were so close"

"I know child"

"What was that?"

"I believe it was the demon Azrul"

"That looked and felt like the shadow figure from the cemetery years back"

"He likes to interfere and he tries to take hold of us witches. It appears he has Catherine and doesn't want to let her go"

"But he came to me one night"

"What do you mean, came to you. Like in a dream?"

"No. I was trying to reach Catherine and he appeared. But he wasn't a shadow. He was in human form. In fact, he was actually rather nice"

"By yourself? You tried to reach her by yourself?"

"Well yeah, but it didn't really work"

"You should never practice such powerful spells alone my dear"

"Nothing happened really. But he did appear in human form. I thought I already mentioned this to you"

"My mind isn't what it use to be deary. If you did, I don't remember. But promise me you'll never try anything like that alone again" I was determined to free my great great grandmother from Azrul's grasp. I had to do some more digging even if it meant going deeper into witchcraft than I really wanted to go. I'll call upon Azrul myself and make him an offer. One he simply can't refuse. Then, I'll have my grandmother back.

Nine

The next night I had prepared a small spell that I would do myself. I had decided to call upon Azrul and trade my life out for Catherine. If he would release her to us now then he could have, in return, my soul when I die. It was a simple made up spell. One that would bring him forth but that he could do no harm while in my presense. I closed up shop early and sent mom home. Told her that I had some inventory to do. That way no one would worry or try to stop me. I then began to get everything ready to say my spell. Placed my 8 black candles around me. My clovers to the side of me for extra protection then said a protection spell. But this time, I added some extra words. Words that would hold Azrul and keep him from doing harm. Words and wisdom usually just come to me when I'm working on my spells. Tillie says it's because all the great witches before me are working through me. I said my protection spell then went straight into the spell to bringing forth Azrul.

"Demon Demon, hear me now. Show yourself Azrul. Be present, be here but bring forth no fear. In place you stand. Feet like stone. No harm will come to any or all known" I said it only once and Azrul did appear. Standing there in front of me without saying a word. I was impressed, I must say.

"I knew I would see you again" he says with a smile on his smug face.

"What is it I can do for you Gabriella?"

"I want you to release Catherine"

"Release her? I do not have her"

"Release her and I'll give you something in return. Something in which you cannot refuse"

"Intrigued, I am. But what is it that you could possibly have for trade to take the place of Lady Catherine Vonness?"

"So you do have her? I knew it"

"Tell me child. I'm curious"

"Me" I say.

"You?"

"I am Lady Catherine's great great granddaughter. I come from a long line of very powerful witches. I could be of great use to you when I'm gone"

"Gone? You could be of great use to me now"

"I don't see how"

"it's simple. If I need you then you help"

"Simple. I've heard of you. It's never simple" He smiles then tries to move closer to me, but he can't. He looks down to his feet. Trying to move them.

"What has happened? What have you done?"

"Ahh. You mean that? You're just being held in place for a bit"

"Held? by what?"

"By me"

"But how? No witches spell has ever been strong enough to hold"

"Yeah see, I'm no ordinary witch. And that's why I offer you a trade. My life, when I'm gone, for my grandmothers"

"I'll give you Lady Catherine but I do want something in return. And not after you're gone. I'm gonna need it now" Hesitate at first, but I knew this could be the only way of getting Catherine.

"OK, name it"

"You have to release me on Earth, but in order to do that, you will need to give blood for blood"

"No deal. I'm not releasing you"

"Then I'm afraid we have no deal"

"Wait, if I release you, what will happen? Like, what will you do?"

"Why whatever I so please, but don't worry. Harm will not come to anyone you know"

"What do you mean by harm?"

"I mean, you're family and friends will forever be safe from me"

"And just how do I release you, exactly?"

"It's simple really. You'll just need to give to me the blood of a living human being"

"The blood?"

"Yes, but it does have to be from someone you hold dear. That way the sacrifice means something"

"Sacrifice? Wait. I didn't say I'd sacrifice for you"

"Then I'm afraid I can't hand over your grandmother" Took a moment to think it over and again knew that this was my only way of releasing Catherine.

"Fine. How do I do this?"

"Good. Now like I said, it must be someone of importance. You have someone in mind?"

"No I don't have someone in mind. It's not like I woke up this morning planning on sacrificing someone I know"

"Well you must find someone soon. My offer only last til midnight tomorrow night" Those were his last words then he vanished.

"But wait, What do I do when I've found someone?" But it was too late. He was already gone. Who could I possibly hand over to Azrul now? Someone that means something to me but also someone I could live without? The only person that came to mind was Chrissy. I love her almost like a sister but honestly, I could go on without her. But how do I go about this? Chrissy probably doesn't even want to talk with me right now. I could just compel her to come to the shop. That way she wouldn't resist it and I could avoid a struggle. I worked on some potions just in case things went awry and left the shop closed the next day so I'd have no interruptions. Got up early and headed on in. But waiting for me at my shop door was Tillie.

"Hey, what brings you here so early?" I asked her.

"Inside child" she says while pushing me through the door.

"What's up?"

"What have you done child?"

"What are you talking about?"

"I felt it last night. Something dark was upon this Earth" Just then I could tell that she could see it all over my face.

"I had to Tillie"

"Had to what?"

"I found a way to bring Catherine back"

"What did you do?"

"I made him an offer and he accepted it"

"Who is he? Don't say Azrul"

"I had to Tillie. This is our only way"

"What did you offer him?"

"Me"

"I won't let you do it"

"I won't let you stop me. Tillie, this is the only way of bringing her back"

"At what cost though Gabriella? It's not worth it. I have told you about giving into the demon"

"It's OK. He promised no harm to me or my family. To anyone I know"

"And you believed him?"

"I had to. It's the only way. But there is one more thing"

"Don't tell me, a sacrifice?"

"How'd you know?"

"I told you about Mordilla"

"Oh yeah"

"Well since I can't stop you. I'm not going to try. So who are we sacrificing and when?"

"We?"

"If you're going to go through with this then I'm going to help you. Maybe then he'll have no power over you with two witches casting"

"Thank you Tillie" So Tillie and I set out on getting Chrissy to the shop and making all preparations for this to go as smoothly as possible. I cast a small spell that compelled Chrissy to come to the shop. When she arrived she just kinda stood at the front door in a haze. Tillie felt her presence and let her inside.

"I'm not sure I can do this Tillie"

"You need to decide that now before this goes any further. Once there's blood there's no going back"

"OK, let's just get it started so this can be over soon" Chrissy stayed motionless. Just staring off in space. Which was better for me. We set up our candles. Placed Chrissy inside a seperate circle created by hemlock and white candles. The sacrifice would be done by a spell. Nothing messy. But i wanted to make sure it was done right. So we called once again on Azrul. Using the same spell that I used before to hold him. He appeared to us.

"I knew you would do the right thing" he says. He looks over to Chrissy.

"Ahh, young Chrissy. She'll do just fine" he says.

"How do you know her name?" I ask.

"There isn't much I don't know Gabriel"

"Let's just get this over. What do we do now?"

"First, you release the hold" he says while pointing to his feet.

"Not gonna happen. The release comes after I have my grandmother. Now, how do we do the sacrifice?"

"Well, you must do it. You will present her to me. Then I'll release Catherine and you will go on to live a happy healthy life" Tillie and I look to one another.

"I'll do it child"

"No Tillie. I have to do it" I take out a small piece of paper containing the spell we came up with to take poor Chrissy's life. I read it out loud while I watched my friend slowly gasp for air. I turn to Tillie.

"It's supposed to be quick and painless"

"It'll be over soon child" Tillie says. Then Chrissy falls to the floor. Azrul takes in a deep breath then again points to his feet. I release the hold and he walks over to her. He tries to reach for her but he can't enter the circle.

"First, my grandmother"

"Yes" he says then just points over to the corner.

"Grandmother" I run to her.

"What did you do Gabriel?" she says. We embrace one another as Tillie removes the spell from Chrissy's circle so Azrul can consume her soul.

"Why my child? You have no idea what you have done"

"It's OK grandmother I'll take care of everything" Azrul took in poor Chrissy's soul then he turned to us "Good day ladies" he says then vanishes away into thin air.

"Not that I'm not forever grateful for what you've done for me but you don't know the hell that you've unleashed upon this Earth"

"I know grandmother, but this was the only way to bring you back. Tillie and I worked day and night on trying to find an easier way but nothing worked. And that's because Azrul had ahold of you. But he don't now. And we did that. Tonight, we changed history. We've made it to where a witch can come back after death. To me, that's worth it. Whatever Azrul throws at us later, then I think we can face him together and beat him. After all, I held him in place" "But how?"

"You see Catherine" Tillie says.

"Your great great granddaughter is unlike any of the other witches. Including yourself. She has power so grand. She writes her own spells. Spells that hold way more punch than any of mine ever have"

"So it is true then?" Catherine asks.

"What's true?" I say while looking to both. Tillie turns to me.

"The prophecy dear"

"The one Mordilla was talking about? Wait, so that means that I'll turn out evil?" Tillie smiles at me then grabs ahold of my hands.

"No child. You are not evil. You have too much good in you. And besides, if you start to feel any darkness then you can fight it"

"I can, how?"

"You proved tonight that you have greater power than evil. You held Azrul, the most powerful demon. No witch has ever been able to do so. You were stronger than him"

"That's true" Catherine joins in. "Matilda's right Gabriel. You've already went further than any of us have. I think you'll be just fine. And I'm so proud to call you my great great granddaughter" I was beyond happy to have Catherine here but now I had to bring her home and introduce her to the rest of the family. Getting home, I find mom passed out on the couch covered with a tiny throw and TV quietly playing an old black and white movie. Which mom loves. Hadley must have stayed at a friend's house and dad was working late. We walk on in and I quietly walk over to my mother. I tap her gently to wake her.

"Gabby, Hey. I must've dozed off"

"Mom, I want you to meet someone" Catherine walks a little closer to us.

"Who's this dear?" mom asks.

"This is Catherine" I say. She smiles at mom.

"Well hello" mom says then "Who is she dear?" she asked again.

"Catherine is family. She is my great great grandmother. She's your great grandmother mom" Mom sits up in her seat more and looks her over.

"But how Gabriel?"

"She had a baby girl named Abigail Rose, that she gave away"

"My grandmother? But how is she here? Wouldn't she be?"

"Dead?" I say.

"Yes, and she was, sorda. But Tillie and I brought her back"

"But she looks so young. Just about my age"

"Cause that's when she died" I say then turn to Catherine.

"How did you die anyhow?"

"It's a long story. One we'll have to save for another day" Mom was just as happy as I was to have Catherine here. We spent the next few days just catching up. Catherine told us all kinds of stories as we did her. Mom took her shopping so she would fit in with today. Everything seemed to be going fine. No sign of Azrul or anything dark. Although Chrissy's mom had reported her missing so the police were asking questions all around town. They didn't think anything serious of it though since Abel just broke off their engagement. Everyone just assumed that she left town a while to clear her head. Which bought me more time to come up with something. I could erase her from everyones memory or just create a spell to make people think she was alright. I could show up at her moms house and appear as Chrissy just to tell her that she's fine but will be going away a while. Then no one would worry at least a little longer. It did bother me that I did what I did but it truly was the only way of bringing Catherine back. I couldn't let the guilt eat at me. I just had to go on. And that's what I did. Abel had came to see me at the shop. It had been a few days and I was starting to miss him. He had been helping his dad at work which gave me time to focus on Catherine. Things were getting pretty serious with us. In fact, he had been talking of marriage. After all, we've known each other all our lives, so it's not like we were rushing. I personally think it was his hormones talking, but hey, can't say that I blame the guy. We were both very attracted to the other and both planned on waiting til marriage. I'm just glad that it was all working out finally.

Catherine stayed with Tillie and they both worked on new potions and spells. Anything to get Catherine back at it. After all, It's been some years since she's said or even heard a spell. We all kept on sharing as much knowledge and memories that we could. I'd say both, Catherine and I were learning new powerful spells. Things in Woodland Grove were really turning out quiet nicely. Fall was here and Halloween was right around the corner. I had planned a big party again for Hadley and my birthday at the shop. We invited the whole town again since everyone seemed to like the Delaney family and frequented the shop often. It was all going good til a few unwanted guest arrived. Yep, you guessed it, Azrul and Mordilla. In walks the two like they own the night. Dressed in 1800's garb as usual. Tillie immediately sensed their presence and headed straight for them.

"Be gone" she days to them.

"You are not welcome here"

"Relax Matilda. Mordilla and I just want to wish the birthday girl a happy birthday and give her a gift"

"She wants nothing from the two of you"

"Let's let her answer for herself" he says just as I approach them.

"Who invited the two of you?"

"Like I need an invitation. Come on Gabriella. You and I are connected now"

"Like hell we are. Neither of you are welcome here, so you need to leave"

"We'll be going, but first, here" he says as he hands over a tiny red box with a black ribbon. "I don't want it"

"I'm sure you'll change your mind"

"I wont"

"Take it. It will, how shall I say this? It will benefit you greatly in the near future. The very near future" I look at the box sitting in the palm of Azrul's hand. A part of me was curious but also a little uneasy about taking something from a demon.

"Don't fall for it Gabriella. That's how he works. He'll just keep pulling you in" Tillie says.

"I have to Tillie" I say then take it from him. He smiles to Mordilla and while looking at her says "We should be going now" Then directed his attention back to me.

"I do hope you have a wonderful birthday and get all you wish for" He and Mordilla then turn and leave. Leaving Tillie and I there just looking at the tiny red box. Tillie grabs it from my hand and heads towards the back of the shop.

"Tillie wait" I follow after her. Catching her just before she tosses it into the garbage. I grab it back from her.

"I have to know what it is. Besides, he said it could help us in the near future. What if he's right? What if there's something in here that we'll need?" I say while holding it.

"OK" she says.

"But before you open it we need to do a cleansing. Just in case he packed a spell in there. It'll protect you long enough to destroy it" We head out the back door of the shop to have some privacy. Tillie did her cleansing then handed it over to me.

"Go ahead. Let's see what's inside" I slowly began to open it. Removing the black ribbon first. It was a tiny locket. A heart shaped brass locket that looked old. I couldn't open it though. What did it mean? Why give this and what could it do to help us? Just then Catherine comes looking for us.

"There you two are. I've been looking for you" she says. Then suddenly her eyes notice the locket.

"Where did you get that?" she asked.

"You know what this is?" She looks at it a moment then takes it in her hand.

"This was mine. I lost it long ago, the night of the fire. I thought I'd never see it again. Have you always had this?"

"Actually no. It was just given to me tonight"

"By who? Tillie?" she asks while looking her way.

"Not Tillie"

"Then who? Your mother?"

"No. It was actually" This is where Tillie interrupted me.

"It was just found at the front door. No tag or anything. We don't know where it came from"

"Really?" Catherine says. As I'm looking in confusion to Tillie. "Come on" Tillie says.

"Let's get back to the party" We start heading back in when Tillie leans in to me and says "I'll explain later. We don't know why it was given to you. Let's just work on figuring out. For now, Let's enjoy the party" Tillie was right. We didn't know anything about the locket or why Azrul gave it to me. And more importantly, said it would be of great use to us in the near future. I'd enjoy our party for tonight then learn as much as I could about the locket tomorrow.

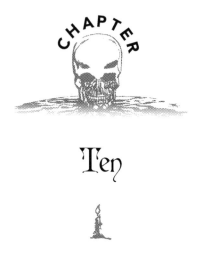

Ten

Morning came and I rose early. Filled in my head were thoughts of this locket and what exactly it's purpose was. Tillie had a point though on not telling anyone including Catherine the truth of where it came from. We didn't have any answers yet as to why Azrul gifted it to me. After all, it once belonged to Catherine and she did just spend quiet a few years with him. Did he know something that we didn't? I'll just hold safe to this locket until we can find out more information on it and why I was now its proud owner. I quickly got ready and headed on into the shop, but first I stopped by the local library just to see if I could find anything at all on the locket and maybe even a bit more info on Azrul. He was a very well known ancient demon. One who preys upon the helpless or mostly those who are seeking revenge, Like Mordilla. She was now like his pet or something. She seemed to do whatever he asked of her. Would this become my fate? Am I also going to be known as a demons puppet? Tillie thinks I have the power to out smart him. I was the only witch to have ever cast a spell on him that took hold. I must say he was very intriguing though. He seemed to fasinate me a lot. Gathered up my papers of information that I had printed out at the library then went on in to the magic shop. Mom had already opened and had a visitor as I entered. Standing by the counter chatting her up was Azrul. Mordilla of course was close by. She's prowling around the shop looking curious.

But you could tell that she wasn't very happy with being there. He turns to me with a smile and a nod.

"Good morning Gabriella" he says. Mom looking a bit curious herself.

"Gabby, honey, your friend was just asking about you" she says.

"My friend?" I say then direct my attention to him.

"Is that what you're calling yourself Azrul? Demon of darkness? Or should I say demon of death?" He seems not at all taken by that remark.

"Whatever do you mean? I have told you Gabriella, I am no demon"

"Really?" I say then toss over my new findings from this morning.

"What's this?" he says as he reaches for a paper.

"This is who you really are"

"This? This is your proof? Who even wrote all this monstrosity?" I take him by the arm and lead him away from the counter and my mother.

"You told me that I wouldn't see you again. That me nor my family would have any trouble from you"

"Yes, and I stand true to my word"

"Yet here you are. In fact, you are everywhere. You keep showing up. Why?"

"You see Gabriella, I'm here because of you. I cannot leave because of you."

"But I don't understand. I was going to go on with my life and you were to do the same. Why won't you just leave?"

"You are afraid? But why? Of what, me? I did promise to not harm you nor will I ever. I only want to see you happy. I am, how do you say it, your protector. Your guardian angel if you will"

"My what? protector, guardian angel, you?" I say with a laugh.

"You call yourself MY guardian ANGEL? You are no angel and I need no protection"

"Ahh, but you could. You just never know what will, and I do say will, happen in the near future" "Yeah about that. Obviously you know something that I don't. And what's with this?" I say as I hold out the locket that I pull from my pocket.

"Why did you give me this, and more importantly say that it could help me in the future? This was Catherine's. Why give it to me and not to her? What is its importance?"

"Time will show itself. But in time you will see the faces of those around you. The real faces" Mordilla then comes on over.

"Can we go now? This place is boring" We both look to her. I wanted to do so much more but I didn't. I refrained from doing any harm, today.

"Remember, guardian angel" he says then they both leave the shop. Mom comes over.

"What was all that? And who is he really Gabby?"

"It's a long story mom"

"Well I've got the time, spill" Mom and I had a heart to heart, in a way, that morning. I told her all about Azrul and how I actually got Catherine back. She wasn't very happy about any of it.

"I really wish that I had already known who he was. I wouldn't have allowed him to stay"

"No, it was probably for the best that you didn't know. I mean, we don't know what would have happened if you said or did anything. He does promise to do no harm to any of us but you just never know" I went about my day trying to focus on just being a normal person for one day at least. But I was finding it really hard. Everywhere I looked I saw Azrul. Everything that I read seemed to remind me of him. Like he was stuck in my head, but why? I'm thinking it's just some link that we have since I am the one to bring him back. To release him onto this Earth. I did have a fascination with him but I felt nothing but anger and wrath for Mordilla. She had to go. Mordilla also is the one who tried to dispose of me earlier at my shop before I released Azrul. Maybe I could talk him into ridding Mordilla from my sight. After all, we are linked and he is here to protect me, so he says. Went out that night with Abel. Wanted some bit of normal. It seemed that all this witchcraft was taking over my entire life. I did nothing really but think of demons, witches, spells, anything to do with my powers growing. I was becoming more stronger with each day passing.

Tillie was now learning new spells from me. Was this so? Did I now, become the teacher? I had already proven that I had the power to contain a very powerful demon. One that none of the witches so far, have ever been able to hold. I also now seemed to be linked to this same demon. Maybe this could be very useful to me in my near future or maybe this could be the start of my downfall. We would soon find out. My night out with Abel was turning out quiet nice actually. It did take my mind off Azrul and Mordilla. Abel and I were growing closer with each date. As if that were even possible. We were already so close. Growing up as best friends and sharing all of life's mysteries with one another kept us the closest of any I know. We had our disagreements from time to time but we always saw through them. We were both wanting and ready to take this to the next level. That night he had proposed to me and I of course said yes. We were sitting in his car. Nothing fancy. Just pulled into my driveway actually and just as I reached for my door handle he takes a hold of my left arm.

"Wait" he says. I turn to him, look at him and wait to see what he had to say. He swallows hard while looking down at his feet then turns to me.

"I don't know why this is so hard, but"

"It's ok. Just breath" I tell him while caressing his cheek.

"Gabby, you know I love you and that you mean everything to me."

"Yeah"

"We've experienced pretty much everything together so far. I want to experience the rest with you."

"And I you Abe"

"What I'm saying is that, that I want to experience, Gabby" He says as he's turning his body fully around to me.

"Gabriella Elizabeth Delaney"

"Yeah" I say with a somewhat muffled voice.

"Will you marry me?" He's looking me dead in my eyes for what felt like forever but I know it could have only been a second or two cause marrying my best friend Abel was all I've wanted to do for years now.

"Yes, absolutely yes I'll marry you" He smiles one of the biggest smiles that I had ever seen him smile then we both grab and hold. I never wanted to leave that moment. It was a moment that I will always remember. I can still feel his warmth. I left his car probably the happiest girl in Woodland Grove that night. As I entered I kept that smile on my face as I strolled past my loving family and went straight upstairs to my room. Hadley comes busting in.

"Hey, you don't say hello anymore?" she says.

"Oh Hadley, the best thing happened to me tonight"

"Let me guess? He finally did it? Abel got the nerve and asked you to marry him? Or be Mrs. Abel whatever you guys do" she's laughing but not actually being serious. But she could tell by the look on my face.

"Wait. Did he, ask you tonight?" I just shake my head in a yes.

"You're for real?"

"For real" She jumps off the bed and yells out the doorway and into the hall.

"Mom, get up here. Wait til you hear what Gabby has to tell you" mom comes strolling in.

"What is so exciting you two?" I look at her and pat the corner of my bed.

"Come, sit. You'll want to sit for this" I tell her.

"Oh Lord Gabby, are you pregnant?" she asked.

"Mom, no. Seriously"

"Well. You've been spending a lot of time away from the house. I don't know what you've been up to"

"Mom, I'm still a virgin. I thought you knew. I told you that I didn't plan on having sex until I got married"

"Yeah but things happen honey"

"Not with me they don't. I meant it"

"OK then, what is so important?" we all sit on my bed and looking so excited, I could tell that Hadley was about to spill if I didn't.

"Abel asked me to marry him tonight. And I said yes"

"Really honey? I think that's wonderful" she says. Then Hadley gets up, walks over to me, grabs my hand and says "Where's the ring?" I look at my hand then pull it back.

"Well, he didn't give one yet. But that's not important. I don't need some flashy piece of jewelry to declare our love. We can grab something later. I'm just happy that he picked me"

"I am happy for you honey. You and Abel have always been there for each other. I remember not long ago you chasing him around the back yard with a stick. Telling him that girls are just like boys, and that they can do whatever they can" We all laugh. She's right. We've always been together. No matter what. Both mom and Hadley go to leave the room when Hadley turns to me "Whatever happened to Chrissy? I mean, I know that you said he called it off with her, but why exactly? And where is she?"

"It just wasn't meant to be for them, and she left town I think. Needed to get away from Woodland"

"Well. I'm sure she'd be really surprised to find out that you two are now engaged" she says then walks on out. Ahh, Chrissy. I did miss her and I hated myself for what I had to do, but I believe that things will work out. I'm still getting to know Catherine more and hoping that it wasn't a mistake in bringing her back. After all, now I have her, Azrul and Mordilla to deal with. I needed to know why Azrul gave me this locket and what was in it? I still hadn't been able to get it open. After everyone left my room I had planned on calling upon Azrul. I needed some answers. I did a small protection spell just in case then said a few words that should bring him here to me. It did in fact. He stands just in front of my window looking puzzled but also a bit happy to see me. He's smiling as to his usual.

"Gabriella. What brings me here?" he ask.

"I do. I need some answers"

"I see"

"We can't keep dancing around this locket. If you know something is going to happen then you need to tell me. That way I can be ready"

"Ready? Yes, you should and you will be, ready"

"See, that. Stop talking like that. Just tell me what it is already."

"You see" he says, then stops. He goes to walk away from the window. He notices that he can. I did not put a holding spell or anything. He nods and smiles.

"You will have what it takes in here" he says while pointing to his chest.

"In where?"

"Your heart Gabriella. You have a pure heart"

"And, how's that going to help?"

"When the time comes to fight evil. You will know what to do"

"But that still don't answer my question. What do you know?"

"I know that your grandmother is not who you think she is?"

"My grandmother, what does this have to do with Catherine?"

"You see, you humans see me as the evil, but like I have already said, I am not evil, nor am I a demon"

"But everything I've read about you confirms it"

"Yes, I'm sure they have written into history some enchanting stories of me. But that is all they are, stories. I am just a poor farmer's son. We had no food, no water, barely clothing on our backs. I watched my father break himself day after day for nothing. He could never take care of his family. So that is when I saw that I had to do something. I was young, naive. I was around 9 years of age when I set out for help. Help that I was sure would be there. Maybe in the next house, the next village, but it never was. No man wanted to help a poor farmer's son. They kicked me. Threw stones at me. Laughed in my face. But as I was wiping my dirty face from the tears that were falling and trying to find my way back home. I came across a very beautiful lady. She smelled nice. In fact, I smelled her before I even saw her. When she topped over the hill and came on up to me. She did not run, nor laugh. Nor did she poke fun of my ragged clothes but instead she knelt down, reached out her hand and touched my face. She gently stroked it while I looked upon hers.

"There there" she said.

"You will come with me" she took me by the hand and we walked back out the path to where we came to a small cottage with a warm fire burning. We get inside and she points over to a wooden chair by the table.

"Sit" she says. I take my seat and she begins to poor me bowl after bowl of the best tasting soup I had ever eaten. It was my first bite of food actually that I had had in weeks. She never judged nor questioned me. She just knew that I needed help.

"I'm sorry that you had to go through that but what's that got to do with Catherine or the fact that you are a demon?"

"The beautiful lady you see, was Catherine"

"Catherine? So then, she's the one who helped you? How does that make her bad?"

"I stayed with Catherine from then on out. She took care of me. Taught me how to survive, but everything changed when, when I saw her for the first time"

"Saw her?"

"I saw Lady Catherine Vonness for who she really was and she didn't like that. I was about 16 and I had made my way into town like I normally do to gather up some new loaves of bread, some grain and a few other things on her list, but I came back a bit earlier than I normally would. I found the door ajar and a strange odor coming from inside. I placed the satchel of goodies just to the side on the ground, then I slowly pushed the door open. I saw nothing out of the ordinary at first so I quietly made my way on through to reach her doorway. It was shut so I hesitated at first, but then I began pushing it open. As I did I could start to see an image. The warm odor was getting stronger as I opened her door more. I saw what looked like a man lying on the floor. I continue looking across the room to see two women on the bed. The man had blood all around him. The women were naked and seemed to be swaying about while holding something over their head and letting whatever it was drip all over them."

"What was it?"

"Blood. It was a large knife and blood was dripping from it. They then finally noticed that I was standing there. One looked at me, it was Catherine. She held out her hand and told me to come to her. I shook my head no, but she just kept saying COME. I finally yelled the words NO and I ran out of the house. I began running into the woods and I just kept running. I ran all night. When morning came I woke in my bed. I wasn't for sure how I got there but Catherine was standing over me. She smiled down at me and gave me a glass of water. I drank then sat up. She then leaned down to me and this is when I saw a dark from inside her that I had never seen. She told me that I was never to mention what I had saw nor was I ever permitted to leave the house unless otherwise told. From that moment on things would never be the same."

"I don't understand. I thought Catherine was good. You're making it out to be that she was evil"

"Is evil. Your great great grandmother was an extraordinary witch. She was an exceptional woman but inside her grew an evil darkness that no one could see coming. She had me fooled for years"

"So how does this lead to you becoming who you are?"

"Ahh yes, I stayed inside the tiny cottage only heading out if I was told to. I minded my own then, a young girl crossed our path. She had traveled into town looking for work. Her father had just passed and her mother was gravely ill. She came to our tiny cottage hoping that we could give her work to earn some food for her and her mother. I met her first outside. She came across the field one evening as I was out gathering up herbs for Catherine. She merely took my breath away she was so lovely. I tried to send her away. For I knew the welcome that she would receive from Catherine, but before she could go Catherine appeared. She saw us talking and came out to greet the young girl. She carried such beauty with her. She was around my age with long golden hair. Face so pure with freckles on her cheeks. I have to say that I was taken by her beauty. Catherine insisted that she stay. She invited her in for some tea and warm bread. She stayed for a few days. Catherine gave her some work to do around the house. She helped with tending to the clothes and gathering up herbs and spices and Catherine promised to give her something in return. But that something that she had in mind was not at all what the young girl had planned. After a long day of gathering and everyone talking and having a good time we ended up in the house sitting by the fire while the girl, thinking she was going to get her pay then head on home to her mother, was wrong. Catherine told me to go into town to get some items that she put on a list, but I didn't want to leave. For I knew that if I did then the girl would not be heading home to see her ill mother. I tried to stay but Catherine insisted. I remember looking at the girl. Taking in all I could. Her face so white and pure. Bright blue eyes and her hair just nestled into a bun barely holding on. I smiled her way before heading out the door. Then I went. Knowing that I would never see her again"

"Then why did you leave?"

"I was young, helpless. I ached inside wanting to help but I knew that if I tried Catherine would probably do something to me. So I was a coward. I left and I was right. On my return I looked for her. Not long, cause inside I already knew, but I did look. I ran inside when I reached the cottage. Only to find Catherine sitting in a rocking chair by the fire. She had in her hands a locket"

"Locket?"

"She had in her hands a locket and she was singing something quietly while rocking. I asked her when I entered, where is the girl? She kept rocking and singing while holding that locket. So I asked her once more. Where is she? She then stopped with her rocking and singing and looked up at me. But when she looked, she moved her head in such force and her eyes were dark. The fire from the fireplace went out and she kept her gaze upon me. I knew then, that she took her life. I knew that Catherine was not the person that I thought she was when she found me that night and brought me home"

"What did she do to the girl?" I asked.

"She sacrificed her to a dark power. So she could live long and keep her beauty"

"Wait, So is the locket you gave me, the one from your story?"

"It is"

"But why give it to me?"

"I kept Catherine contained for so many years but now that you released her back to this Earth you'll need something to hold her again"

"And the locket, it'll do that?"

"It will"

"How?"

"You see it's not just a locket. It's full of dark magic. That's why she yearns for it"

"I still don't see how it will hold her or keep her from being evil"

"The locket belongs to an ancient warlock named Maleek. He held such dark sorcery. It was a very magical locket that, with it, you held such great power. Anything that your heart desired would come true."

"How did Catherine get the locket?"

"She came across it one night while in the desert. She was traveling with a few others and times were getting hard. She found it lying on the bottom of a creek bed while washing her face one day. Not knowing it's true meaning she still took it. For it was a lovely piece of jewelry that she just could not take her eyes off. It's like it speaks to you. She took the locket and held on to it for a few more months. Then when things got really hard she started praying to the Gods. Any God really. Anyone that would hear her plea and answer. Well, Maleek heard and he answered. But once you give in to darkness then, then you will eventually become that darkness. And Catherine did. She got all that she wanted and when she didn't, then there was hell to pay. To keep her young and beautiful she would have to sacrifice the young and beautiful now and then. And that's what she did with the young girl that evening."

"So, if it helps her, then how will it stop her?"

"Because young Gabriella. It gives your heart's desire for the one who owns it."

"So, if I wish her to be good and not evil, then she'll be good?"

"Exactly"

"But why did you give it to me? Why not just keep it for yourself?"

"I have no use for it any longer. Besides, you have proven that you are far more powerful than I. So if anyone is going to stop her then it needs to be you" I was beginning to wonder if I had done the right thing on bringing Catherine back. She didn't seem to be evil though. And she never pushed for me to bring her back. This was all my idea. So maybe Azrul was right. Maybe since I wish her to be good then maybe she will be. Only time would tell. I had been busy planning my upcoming wedding that I didn't really think too much on Catherine and all that Azrul had said. I did keep it in the back of my mind though. I wanted a Summer wedding and something outside. I loved nature and all the pretty flowers. Abel and I picked a spot out by the river. It was beautiful. There was a wooden walkway that lead out to a gazebo over the water. There were already beautiful plants growing everywhere but of course I'd have to add more, way more. We were planning on the end of August. I couldn't wait really. We had waited long enough and everything was falling right into place lately. While out shopping for some little odd and ends Hadley and I bumped into an old friend. Well, I wouldn't really call her a friend. We saw Amiyah Liam's girlfriend. I had wondered what everyone was up to lately since I never really did see anyone from school anymore. She was the first to say hey. As we're standing there looking through fake flowers she turns the corner.

"Well if it isn't Gabby. How you been?" she asked.

"Amiyah. Hey"

"Is this little Hadley?"

"It sure is"

"Not so little anymore huh. Well it sure is nice to see some familiar faces. What have ya'll been up to?"

"Not much. Just running the shop"

"I heard about that. You have a magic shop is it? Mom told me about that. How's that going?"

"Good actually. So, you back in town?"

"I am. Liam lost his job with the paper so we decided on trying it back here. His dad got him on at the factory"

"That's good. So, you and Liam?"

"Yep." she says as she holds up her hand to show off a shiny big diamond.

"Wow. That's nice. I'm actually here looking for some finishing touches for my wedding"

"No kidding. Anyone I know?"

"Yeah actually. It's Abel"

"Abel Finch?"

"The one and only"

"That's great. You guys have known each other forever huh?"

"All our lives"

"Well, I won't keep you. It was good seeing you though. We'll have to do something some time."

"Sure" I say with some confusion. After all, we never liked each other or got along. And I'm not sure how I feel about seeing Liam again after all these years. I didn't feel for him anymore. I just think it might seem a little weird to be just hanging out after I did crush on him so hard. And he knew it, everyone knew it. Especially Abel.

We finished up our shopping and headed on out. I dropped off Hadley to her boyfriends then I took a drive on over to the cemetery. I didn't visit there as much anymore since I had so much on my plate lately. But figured I could use a little quiet time. I get there. Park my car and I see someone standing over in front of a tombstone. Not sure who it was at first so I stayed my distance. But when I got a little closer I noticed it was a girl. She looked young. Blonde hair, pale skin. I didn't recognize her so I tried not to disturb her. I stayed over to the side and sorda walked around a bit. I looked back and she was gone. I looked through the cemetery but I never did find her. I even walked back towards my car to see if someone was in the driveway but no one was there. So I'm assuming that it was a ghost then. There one minute then gone the next. I just took it as that and went about my night. When I got home there was the same girl again, sitting on my doorstep. I get out, go up to her.

"Hello" I say.

"I saw you earlier at the graveyard right?" I asked. She looks up to me and then begins to cry. She places her face in the palms of her hands. "What's the matter?" I asked. "You can tell me. You're not real, I know. I mean, you're a ghost. I'm use to seeing your kind" She stops crying then looks up at me. Her face turns dark and eyes red. She stands to her feet.

"You will know pain like you've never known before. Suffering will come to you in many forms. I have spoken these words of which will come to you by nigh of the next full moon" She then disappeared into a thousand black birds that flew away into the night sky. What just happened? Was this Mordilla again? Who was this girl and why did she say those horrible words to me? I immediately called Tillie and asked her to come over. I wasn't for sure what to do about this one. I was even afraid to drive anywhere now. Tillie arrived and finds me pacing back and forth on my front porch.

"Slow down child. Explain to me exactly what she said"

"Tillie this was bad. She was pure evil." I told Tillie what she had said to me.

"Oh dear child. I'm afraid that you have been cursed"

"Cursed?"

"Yes. Cursed"

"By who and why?"

"We need to be finding out and the sooner the better" she grabs me by the arm and leads me inside. She starts gathering up herbs and other items and begins conjuring up spells right there in my kitchen.

"Why would anyone curse me? I haven't done anything to anyone"

"Well someone is pissed. And we need to find out before the next full moon. Which you don't have much time" So there we are scrambling around my kitchen creating potion after potion and trying to figure out who could have placed this curse on me. Tillie did the best anti-curse spell she could, but since the curse was already placed, it could only help with slowing it down. At least that's what we were hoping. While in my kitchen and looking for any help possible a thought came to me, Azrul. Maybe he could help. He said he was my protector so I'll call upon him. I did just that. He shows up as Tillie is throwing almost everything in my kitchen into this huge pot that she is working on.

"Ladies" he says. Then directs his attention to me.

"We keep meeting like this" Tillie looks over to me.

"What does he mean?" she asks.

"Never mind" I say then turn to him.

"I need your help"

"Anything" he says with a smile.

"It appears that I have been cursed" Turning more serious, he looks at me.

"Cursed? Are you sure?"

"Pretty sure"

"Well how do you know"

"Well she said that I will know pain like I've never known before. And that suffering will come to me in many forms and I have until the next full moon. So what do you think?"

"That is most definitely a curse"

"Can you help us then?" I asked.

"I will most certainly try" We all three set out over the next few hours of trying to find out anything we could on who could have placed this curse on me. Azrul went straight to the underworld. He spoke to as many demons that he could. Those that would help anyways. Having no luck he returned to Tillie and I still up at my house going through book after book for anything. None of us were finding anything of any use. Morning was approaching and mom and dad were rising to get their day started. I wanted to spare them any concern so I just told them that we were working on something else. Anything else really. Tillie headed out along with mom and dad. Leaving Azrul and myself there alone.

"You know you never did tell me how you became a demon" I say to him.

"I didn't did I"

"Not really"

"You see, after I began to see Catherine for who she really was and after she took the life of someone that I thought I could be interested in, then I more or less lost hope for humanity. For anything really. I started giving in to all her wicked ways. Became like her dog you could say. If she said fetch then I fetched"

"But why?"

"Why not I guess. I began thinking that this was the way of life"

"So, you turned evil?"

"Not at first. I may have helped Lady Vonness with her wrong doings but I still had a piece of human in me. On the eve of my 21st birthday she took me out to a new town. Said that it was my night. And that I could have anyone that I wanted. She would make sure. So, I scrolled the placed. Looking to every face. Trying to find one that resembled the young pale faced girl from years ago. The one that took my breath away. I came across one girl. She was quiet. Sitting over in the corner drinking on her warm herbal tea. She wanted no part of the party that was all around her. She seemed pure and good. I looked upon her from afar, but I knew that if I said it was her, that Catherine would destroy her. So I began to turn away, but she saw my face. She knew that I had placed my eyes upon that one girl sitting in the corner. She comes closer to me. Leans in with a smile.

"Very well" she says. "I'll bring her to you" she then proceeds to head over to her. She places one hand on her shoulder while whispering in her ear. The young girl smiles at Catherine then gets up from her seat and walks my way. My heart begins to skip a beat. She was beauty and so full of life. She reaches me and kisses me gently on my cheek. We spent the rest of the night talking and getting to know each other. I was so very happy. When morning came and Catherine had found us. She said we were to be leaving by nightfall. That I was to get all that I wanted out of her before then. But I wanted to keep the girl. I wanted to make her mine. Little did I know that Catherine had other plans."

"What happened to her?"

"We were saying our goodbyes and how we planned on seeing each other the next evening when she stopped suddenly. She just couldn't breathe anymore. I looked to Catherine cause I knew it was her. I told her to stop but she didn't. She continued on with what she was doing. Which was taking her beautiful life so she could continue to live long and beautiful"

"Why didn't you stop her?"

"I couldn't. I had no power, then"

"Then what happened?"

"Then I knew that I would no longer let Lady Vonness take another beautiful soul for hers. I had to do something. I went with her that night back to our cottage and I waited for her to fall fast asleep. Then, taking a page from her own book. I took a spell that I had found and I read it out underneath the full moon. Not sure what I was doing or if I was even doing it right, but I had to do something to stop her. I read out loud the words that made me who I am today and gave me the power to stop Catherine from taking the lives of others"

"What did you say exactly?"

"Just a bunch of gibberish really"

"Well that gibberish worked"

"Yeah"

"But what exactly happened to Catherine?"

"Let's just say that she lost most her power that night. The locket was placed in my hands and she was merely just a normal person now"

"So you rendered her powerless?"

"You could say"

"Wow. I'm impressed"

"Really, impressed? The great Gabriella Delaney is impressed by me?"

"Great. I wouldn't go that far. I mean, we are here trying to figure out how to remove a curse that was placed on me. Don't know how great I am"

"Gabriella you are far greater than even you can imagine. There have been foretold stories of you"

"I heard some things. Something about an old warlock Artemis"

"Ahh Artemis, he was a smart man"

"Really now? Cause I'm hearing that he was not in his right mind"

"Oh but that makes for the best stories" We spent the day together trying to find out more on my curse. The style of the curse. The girl that I had send first at the cemetery then at my house. I described her to Azrul and he seemed to think that it was all too weird of a coincidence that the girl I described sounded like his young girl that Catherine had taken her poor soul.

"So you think that it could be her? But why would she place a curse on me?"

"Maybe it's to get back at me"

"Why me though? If she wants to get to you, then why curse me?"

"Witches and Warlocks work in weird ways. They tend to go after the thing that we love or admire the most. Instead of a direct attack on ourselves. It seems to do more damage"

"But still, I don't understand"

"Gabriella you are of great importance to a lot of people"

"So how do we find out who is doing this? And I still don't get it. Why curse me to get back at you?" he looks at me a moment then tries to change the subject.

"I wonder how Matilda is doing on her findings?"

"No, look at me. Why would someone curse me to get back at you? I mean, I'm nothing to you, right? Right?"

"You, are not nothing. You are truly an amazing person and I will help you rid this curse" he says then flips through a book and begins reading out loud. What was his fixation on me? And why would anyone put a curse on me to get to him? Him and I are nothing alike. It's true I was seeing him in a different light now after hearing his story about him and Catherine, but still, he was still considered a demon. We spent a few more hours working on spells to breaking this curse when Tillie and Catherine comes walking in.

"Look who I found" Tillie says as she enters into the kitchen and motions to Catherine.

"You guys have been so busy lately that I hardly ever see you" she says then notices Azrul standing there.

"Why is he here?" she asks.

"He's helping me" I tell her.

"Helping you, do what exactly?"

"Well it appears that I have been cursed"

"Cursed? How do you know this for sure?"

"It was a curse" Tillie assures her.

"By whom?" she asks.

"That we don't know. That's actually what we are trying to figure out and maybe even a way to ease it" I tell her.

"Then why do we need him? For all you know, it was him that placed this curse on you" Catherine says.

"It's not him Catherine" I tell her.

"Well how do you know for sure dear?" We both look at one another a moment then turn to Azrul.

"I just do" I say then smile at him. "Now let's quit standing here talking and get to work. I am cursed ya know and there is a time frame" I explain to Catherine the whole story of this girl, what exactly her words were and when I would start to feel the effects. Azrul is getting a bit uneasy about being around Catherine I can tell, but we need him there. I need all them there and working together. Time had passed and it was a little after four pm. Time for mom and Hadley to be getting home.

"We need to hurry guys. If my mother finds out about this curse then she'll lose it" We finish up and clean up all our messes from todays spell session, and just in time. Hadley and her boyfriend come strolling in.

"Hey guys" she says while rushing to the fridge for a glass of milk and then grabs an apple from the counter.

"What's up?" she's looking at all of us with her childlike eyes, waiting for an answer.

"We were just working on some potions. Gotta keep on your toes. Never know when some big bad will be striking" I say then push her on out.

"Hey. I'm well old enough for this stuff. I've seen some of your books. I know what you guys do" Just then mom comes in the room.

"There you are. Honey I've tried calling you all day" she says to me.

"Oh sorry. I've been busy and I just forgot about everything else. Just tuned it out I guess. What did you need?"

"Nothing really. You had a couple visitors at the shop asking for you"

"Oh really, who was it?"

"Liam and his girlfriend, well, I guess it's wife now"

"Liam, no kidding. So, Liam and Amiyah came by. They say anything?"

"No. Just came in to check out the shop and did want to set up a date or time that you guys could get together and do something"

"Yeah, about that" I say as I'm interrupted by Hadley.

"Do something? Are they kidding? The whole town knows how you longed for his affection and hated Amiyah. Pretty much everyone hated Amiyah. Why in the world would you do something with them?" She says with a laugh. Azrul walks over to me, leans in a little, to where only I could hear him and says "You longed for his affection?" I look his way and smirk.

"Not exactly" I tell him.

"Only a fool would not return that affection to you" he says then turns to walk into the other room. I must say that I was really beginning to get puzzled by Azrul's reactions. This man that was supposed to be so evil and full of hatred, was not. He was nothing but nice to me. In fact, a little too nice. We finished up our evening and everyone had went home.

I hadn't got to speak with Abel today so I was missing his sweet voice. Thought I'd pop next door to see if he was in. The lights were all out at his house but I knocked anyways. No answer. I climbed up the side railings to reach his window. Like I had done so many times before. His window was locked. Which was strange cause he never locks his window. I tapped on it a few times but no luck. I guess he's working late with his dad so I'll head back on home. As I entered into my room I saw a dark figure standing over by the window. I tried to turn on my light but it didn't work. I called out "Who's there?" No answer. I said a spell to bring forth light and there appeared a small glow around us. The dark figure turned to me. I could see it a little better but not enough to make out who it was. Still appeared a little blurry and dark around the face.

"What do you want?" I asked. It flickered a few times then softly spoke.

"He who holds the dark will only shield it for so long"

"I don't understand"

"What is inside of us all will eventually make its way out"

"You're not making sense. Who are you and what do you want with me?" I ask a little louder. It then gets deeper and louder itself. While speaking the same words a lot faster now.

"THE DARKNESS INSIDE WILL COME OUT" It says then vanishes out my open window into the dark night. Things were appearing to me a lot more now but now I was not always able to see who it was or what it wanted. Things were also more evil. I turned to my grimoire for answers. Just as I opened it the letter that Tillie had given me years ago with the broach, the one that I couldn't read, fell out. I opened it once more. But this time the words were more clear. I could actually make most of them out. It looks to be a spell of some kind. Guess Tillie was right about me being able to read the old witch language as I grow stronger in my powers. It read "The wind that brings forth the time brings with it a new divide. With faces of beauty. Hair of gold. Skin like honey and lips of rose. I give to you" And that's where it gets a little jumbled and hard to read. It's most definitely a beauty spell of some kind, but at what cost? Could this be it? Could this be the spell that Azrul told me about that Catherine used to sacrifice so she could stay young and beautiful? Could it be that Catherine was trying to pass it on to the next great witch? Cause she thought once she died then she wouldn't need it any longer. I will hide this spell just in case this is that exact spell that Catherine used to take the lives of those innocent young souls. I went straight to bed and fell fast asleep.

The day was long and full of hard work so my body was drained and tired. That night I slept one of the best sleeps that I had had in years. Not sure why. I mean, I had a curse on me and Lord knows what just showed up in my bedroom appearing all mysterious and evil, but I slept like I had not a care in the world. I didn't know it at the time but Azrul was actually watching over me. He had Mordilla place a protection barrier around me. Guess that's what helped me sleep. Now I know that Mordilla was not at all happy about that. For we know that Mordilla hates my guts. So I'm sure that it being from her hand the reason that I was being protected, was just eating her up. When morning came I rose bright and early. Took my shower. Got dressed and ate a rather large breakfast. Even mom and Hadley were surprised. They're all watching me from across the table as I'm stuffing my face with morning goodness.

"Wow Gab" Hadley says.

"Are you feeling ok honey?" Mom asked. I just smile.

"I'm feeling great actually"

"You sure you're not pregnant?" Hadley asked.

"Funny. I'm just hungry this morning. All that potion making yesterday just took it out of me I guess"

"Whatever" Hadley says. You know little sisters. So, this is Hadley's last year of school and I wanted to do something special for her. Plus I had my wedding coming up and I knew that once I married I probably wouldn't get to see much of my lil sis so I really wanted to get that bonding time in. I mean, we were very close sisters. Always have been and I'm sure we always will be. But we were growing up and starting our own lives now. I begin planning a big surprise graduation party that would be here in a few months time. I filled mom and dad in on it but told them to under no circumstances to ever tell Hadley. I wanted it to be a complete surprise. So I was busy, extremely busy over the next few months. I had a wedding to finish planning and getting ready for, my sisters graduation party and of course, I still had a curse to worry about. So, when I say I was busy. Believe me I was busy. Abel helped with the wedding and Hadley's party but I haven't told him yet about this curse on me. I didn't want to bother him. Now I was given a time frame on when I would start to see things happen I guess. It was by the next full moon. Which was about to happen. In like two days to be exact. Tillie still hadn't came up with a spell or potion to break the curse nor had any of us been able to figure out who placed this curse.

One night as I'm sitting at the shop by myself and looking through some old ancient books I came across a photo. It was of an old evil Enchantress named Isadora and underneath her photo were a few scribblings. Something similar to the words that were spoken to me when I was cursed. I jumped to my feet. This is it. It has to be. I mean the words were almost exact. But who was she and why would she want to put a curse on me? I immediately went to Tillie with it. She knew of her of course but she too was puzzled about the why. We called upon Azrul to see if he knew anything about this Isadora. He looked a moment at her photo then placed it back down.

"She is something that neither of you want to mess with" he says.

"If she is the one that did place the curse on you, then, then you will not be able to break it"

"That can't be. I mean I have to. If I don't then, bad things will happen" I say while pacing the room.

"Calm down child" Tillie says.

"I'm sure there is something we can do" she says then looks towards Azrul.

"Maybe offer her something in return. Would that work?" she says while looking at Azrul and awaiting his reply.

"You don't get it. Isadora holds such great power. She sits on a throne of almighty. When she does something she sees it through. She will not remove this curse"

"But why did she place it on me to begin with?" I ask. Both Tillie and Azrul are looking at me.

"Well? This is my life here and I'm not going to just stand here and watch this Isadora destroy it, and for what reason? Why? I don't even know her so it has to be a mistake. I want to talk with Isadora"

"You don't" Azrul says.

"I do"

"You would have no chance"

"We'll see about that" I reach for a spell book and begin looking for a spell to calling out Isadora. I had power and I'm sure that I could do something to stop this curse"

"You don't know what you're up against here Gabriella" Azrul says with all concern.

"You have power, yes. But you are not strong enough to go against Isadora"

"Then you will help. You and Tillie. Even Catherine and Mordilla can if needed"

"Dear I'm afraid he's right"

"No Tillie. We have to do something. I have only two days left. I don't know what's going to happen, and I don't want to find out." They don't want to but Tillie and Azrul set out to helping me call upon Isadora and finding out why she is doing this to me. We also get Catherine and Mordilla to help us. Since this Isadora is so powerful, we needed all the help that we could get. We're there in Tillie's living room. Candles lite and sage a burning. We stand our ground. Firm and ready to get some answers from this evil Enchantress. She appears to us with bolts of lightning around and darkness to follow. She has the darkest eyes and has set them on my sight as soon as she appears. I'm looking at her. She's looking at me. Inside I feel trembling and fear but I won't let her see it. We all wait to see who is going to speak first then I take the chance. I throw at her feet a potion that I had prepared earlier to contain her in her place. I say a few words then I began my questions.

"What do you want with me? Why did you place a curse on me?" I ask and wait for her reply. She looks my way then across to the others then back at me and laughs.

"I have placed no curse on you. I have no need to curse you, a mere mortal" she says.

"Mere mortal. Then you don't know who I am?" I say.

"Oh I do know. You are Gabriella, the holder of great power. The witch who will lead the lost out of the darkness" Well ok. Not really have I been described that way before but I'll take it.

"You did place a curse on me. Did you not?" I ask.

"I did not, but I do admire your courage in calling me out and asking this." I look to Tillie then to Azrul.

"If you didn't, then who?"

"I'm sure, if someone did place a curse then they have all good intentions on doing so" Isadora says.

"Why? I could see if I had wronged someone but I hadn't" And just as I said those words an image appeared to me of young Chrissy and her life being stolen from her by me. But she was only human. No special powers. Could it be her somehow? Isadora looks our way and tells us in the most stern voice.

"Never try to reach me again. For there will be consequences if so" She says then takes her leave. This leaves us all standing there looking to one another.

"OK, then who is it?" Tillie asked. I look to her then to Catherine.

"I think I might have an idea" I say then walk away from them. They follow after.

"Well who child?" Tillie says.

"Maybe it's Chrissy" I say to Tillie. She takes a step back and thinks to herelf.

"I know. She's only human, but" I say then Tillie jumps in.

"No, that could be it. After all, you did take the poor girls life. She could have been approached by a demon for revenge" I look to Azrul.

"Could it be her? When you consume someone, what happens to them?" I ask. He takes a moment then says "I don't see how. I take in that person fully. They are no longer. No soul to reach out to for revenge."

"Then who?" asked Catherine.

"If it isn't Chrissy, then how would we find out? What would we do Tillie?" I asked.

"I guess we could consult Anouk" she says.

"Who's Anouk?" Mordilla steps in.

"He's a fool. A warlock that has tried to become human."

"Become human? What do you mean?" I ask. she begins telling me

"Many years ago Anouk fell in love. He wanted to wed this shy little peasant girl but once she found out that he was a warlock, she wanted no part of him. He did everything he could to rid his powers but it only made him stronger. He became so strong that the darkness took him over completely. Since the peasant girl turned away from him he set out to help anyone that was out for revenge. That was all he saw."

"So then, let's talk to this Anouk" I say. I leave Tillie's house and head back to the shop where Azrul meets back up. "What are you doing here?" I ask.

"You said you were to speak with Anouk"

"Yes"

"Well, let's speak to Anouk."

"I'm sure you have other things to do besides dig up all these old witches and warlocks."

"Not really, besides, I told you guardian angel" he says then smiles.

"Right. Well then, let's get started." I grab my book and look for Anouk. Read up on any information that we had on him. Found a spell that would reach him so I could talk with him. The only problem is that, to call upon him one must be looking for revenge. I didn't have anyone that I disliked at the moment or needed to get my revenge on. If anyone pissed me off then I took care of it myself. So, not sure what I was gonna do here. Azrul thought he had a way. He used Mordilla to call on him since she had plenty that she could get revenge on. We closed the shop and began our spell. In comes Anouk but this time he walks right through the front door. Odd, but not out of the ordinary I guess. After all, powerful warlock here. He walks in as we all just stare at him. Walks over to the table where we are and asks "Which one is Mordilla?" Both Azrul and I look her way.

"Yes" he says.

"I should have known. I can feel the hate coming from inside, but" he says then looks my way.

"Could it be that you hate her so much?" he asked while looking back at Mordilla.

"Whatever do you mean?" she says. He looks at me then to her.

"I can see why. She is lovely and the power" he says while breathing in.

"The power is so strong. You feel jealous."

"I don't know what you are talking bout" Mordilla says. Then looks at me.

"Really, a fool I told you" he turns quickly back her way.

"FOOL? You call me here to exact revenge and you call me the fool?"

"Enough" I say.

"She called you here for me"

"I know" he says.

"Not that way. We called you here because someone has placed a curse on me and I need to find out who it was?"

"And you think I can help? That I will help? What gives you that idea?"

"I had done something to someone that I'm not very proud about, but I needed to at that time. And I need to know if it is she who is doing this" He takes a few steps back then moves the chair away from the table and sits down.

"I know of no one who has set out for revenge on you" he says.

"Are you sure?" I ask.

"I am quiet positive."

"But I don't get it. I just don't under-stand. Who would do this to me?" I stand to my feet and walk out of the room. Leaving Azrul and Mordilla with Anouk.

"There is a way to find out" Anouk tells them.

"How?" asked Azrul.

"It's a simple spell that only she can do"

"Go on."

"By nights end she will need to rid herself of all things humanly possible. She will need to clear her mind and give herself to the" and just then Azrul stops him.

"The demon of the night. She will not" he says.

"Then she will not know who is cursing her" Mordilla comes over to Azrul.

"What is it to you if she gives over herself to this demon?" she asks. he looks st her then back to Anouk.

"Is there another way?"

"Well you can always wait til this curse plays out. Then maybe the one who placed it will show his or herself" he says while looking towards Mordilla again. Azrul notices and immediatley takes hold of her, by the neck.

"Is this you?" he asked while squeezing every bit of air out. She's trying to get words out but cannot. Just then I come back into the room.

"What are you doing?" I say and say a quick spell for him to release her. He loses grip and she falls to the floor. Anouk just laughs. I look at him.

"What? What is so funny?" I say.

"You can't see it can you?" he says.

"See what?"

"In time, you will" he says then he gets to his feet.

"If there is nothing else that you will be needing from me then I shall be leaving" He then leaves the shop and not long after Mordilla follows. I turn to Azrul.

"What happened?"

"Nothing"

"That wasn't nothing. Why were you trying to strangle Mordilla?"

"Just leave it" he says then goes back to the table.

"Did he say something when I left or does she know something? Really Azrul, I'm running out of time here"

"No, I just, I just thought that maybe it was, never mind" I sit down by him.

"You thought what? You thought that it was Mordilla that placed the curse on me? Is that it?" I look at him and wait for his answer. He looks at me then gets up to leave.

"Wait" I say to him.

"Thank you" He turns and looks my way then back towards the door and heads out. What was happening with my life lately? Everything seemed to be spinning and changing. I wouldn't say it was bad, just changing. I should have been more frightened than I was about now only having one more day left until something finally took place. But I wasn't. I feel like I had control. I had enough powerful people around me that I felt, if something bad took place, then we could fix it. By the last day I had spent it all with my family. Mom, dad, Hadley and I went to the movies then grabbed a bite to eat. Afterwards, Abel and I took a walk down by the water and had a small picnic. It was such a terrific day that no matter what happened, I felt I could handle it. By nightfall I was preparing myself, just in case. Both Tillie and Catherine offered to hang around. To even sleep over if needed. But I was sure it was all gonna be alright. I had just jotted down a few things from that day in my journal and was just getting settled into bed when I heard a knock on my bedroom door. Hesitate at first but I managed to get to my feet and see who it was. I opened the door slowly to find Abel standing there holding up a few movies and a pizza. I smile to him, grab him and pull him inside. I gave him the biggest kiss ever.

"Wow" He says.

"I should have showed up at your door long ago I guess."

"Shut up and keep kissing me" I tell him. We spent some time making out then things turn a bit serious. A darkness filled the room. I push him back to the wall for protection. The wind is blowing.

"Gabby, what is it?" he asks. But I'm too focused on what could be in my room at the moment. I now had Abel to protect, not just myself. In fact, I wasn't even worried about me, only him. I'm saying a few words of protection while still trying to see what it was that was circling my room. Everything went so fast. By the time it was over I really didn't know what had just happened. I look around. Nothing seems to have changed. I look over to Abel. Grab hold of him then look him over. Finding nothing I immediately run to my phone and call Tillie. I'm talking too fast to make clear words. She's trying to calm me down but it just don't work. I knew at that moment that the curse was now in full effect. The pain and suffering that had been placed upon me was now going to start showing its ugly face. Now, it was just a waiting game.

Eleven

Abel wanted to stay over but I assured him that everything was going to be fine. I sent him on his way after we said our goodnights and I dug deep into my grimoire. I wanted to study up as much as I could on curses and how to remove them. I may have missed the deadline for all this to start but I could still find out who was doing this and hopefully get it removed. No luck on figuring out who it was but I did find a little spell that could call out hidden attacks Such as this curse. I was to bless this stone that I had and wear it around my neck. Whenever the attacker came near it would glow. Figured it was worth a try. I found a pretty opal that had been handed down to me by my mother. It was something that apparently, has been in the family for quiet some time now. It was kinda small and dainty. Pretty enough to wear everyday. So I fixed it up. Placed it in a bowl of warm water. Filled the bowl with some herbs and black powder. Lite my black candle then said the words.

"From inside this stone I give you power. Power to bring forth those who wish to harm me" I said it twice then crumpled up the piece of paper with the spell on it and threw it into the bowl. Blew out my black candle then waited til nightfall for the spell to take effect. When morning came and I prepared myself for the day. I threw on my new improved opal necklace in hopes that in would in fact, bring out this person who is doing this. Only thing is, I have to be close to them or else the stone wouldn't glow. So, in a way tricky cause that means that my attacker could very well be someone close to me. I didn't see that happening but ya never know. I arrived at the shop and went on inside to find Mom had already opened for me. First thing to catch her eye was my new necklace.

"That's lovely" she says while leaning in to take a closer look.

"Looks familiar"

"Well it should. It was yours" I say.

"Really?"

"Yeah, It's the opal that you gave me on my 13th birthday, remember?"

"Well it is. And you made it into a necklace"

"Yeah, figured it would be something different"

"It's beautiful honey. So, any plans for this coming weekend?"

"Not really. Probably just stay around the house and look through my books."

"Again? Aren't you spending enough time doing that here?"

"You can never spend enough time on witchcraft mom."

"Honestly Gabby, what could you possibly learn now? I mean, you know so much already."

"Oh but there is so much more I want to know."

"Just don't let it consume you dear."

"As if that's possible."

"I'm sure it is. After all, it's taking up so much of your time already"

"Mom, mother. I am a witch, and a very powerful one. Well, at least I could be if I just keep at it. Each day I'm learning something new."

"Yes, and each day you are becoming more distant from your family" she says while flipping over the open/close sign for the door.

"Any word on this curse?"

"I still don't know who is doing it but I'm on it. In fact, that's actually why I have on this necklace"

"Really?"

"Yeah, it's fixed up to tell me if someone comes near, if they are to do me harm. It will glow"

"That's neat"

"Yep, now I just wait." We went about our day and kept things as usual. Kinda slow really. In fact, I hadn't seen Abel, Azrul, Tillie or Catherine. Just pretty much me and mom and a few customers here and there. Come closing time we both finished up and locked up the shop. As I was walking to my car I saw the girl again. Just standing there in between mine and moms cars.

"Wait mom" I say as I hold out my hand to stop her from walking forward.

"What is it honey?"

"It's the girl from before"

"You mean the one who cursed you?"

"Yeah" Just then mom goes walking on up to her to confront her.

"Just who do you think you are?" She's saying but the girl throws up a hand and knocks mom back without even touching her.

"Mom" I yell then go towards her. The girl freezes me in my tracks. "What are you doing? Do you know who I am?" I say. She laughs then focuses her attention on me.

"Do you know who I am?" She says then throws her head back to look towards the sky. The clouds are rolling and thunder is crashing. The wind is blowing hard. She looks back to me. "I am not here to harm you Gabriella. I am here to take you."

"Take me? What do you mean?"

"I am here to show you what you could have. What you could do. If only you would let it in."

"Let what in exactly?" She starts laughing some more then more thunder and clouds are rolling when she moves closer to me and looks me right in the face.

"Let us in" she says then she's gone. Nowhere in sight. I rush over to check on mom.

"Honey, who was that?"

"I'm not sure, but I plan on finding out" We get to our cars and head on home. I told her to drive straight home. I'll be right behind her and not to stop for anyone. On our way I call Tillie and ask her to meet us at my house. I also try to call upon Azrul to see if he could hear me. I try focusing several times in my mind, calling out his name.

"Azrul can you hear me?" I say it several times but only in my mind. Then finally he appears in my front seat. Startled at first, but glad it worked.

"Wow" I say as I look over to him.

"Can't believe that worked" He seems astonished as well. He's looking around to see where exactly he is.

"I'm in your car" he says.

"Yeah, it appears so."

"How?"

"Never mind that. Right now we need to discuss what just happened."

"What just happened?"

"The girl, the same one from the house and the cemetery. The one that placed this curse on me, well she came back."

"She did, where?"

"She showed up at the magic shop."

"What did she say? Are you alright?"

"I'm fine, we're fine, but"

"We?"

"Me and mom. We were closing up and walking out to our cars when she was just standing there. She told me that she wasn't going to hurt me but that she wanted to take me with her."

"Really? How odd"

"I thought so too"

"Then what happened? Did you go?"

"Well no, I'm here aren't I" We look to one another.

"Anyhow, she said something like I could be so powerful if I'd just let them in."

"Who's them?"

"I don't know. That's where you come in. I thought maybe you would know."

"Not really. I mean, I've been out of commission a while now and besides, I told you, I'm not a demon."

"Yeah yeah. Well you must know something or have heard something"

"I can look around. Did she give you a name at all?"

"No. But it was the same blonde girl from earlier. But what I don't understand is, if she doesn't plan on harming me then why did she curse me?"

"That is puzzling. I'll talk to a few people that may know a little something then I'll get back with you."

"Thank you, really. You don't know how much it means that you keep helping me. Here I thought that you were going to be this big bad and you're turning out to be actually really good" he just looks over to me and smiles then he poofs away. I arrive home to find Tillie pulling in at the same time. She comes rushing over.

"What happened child? You sounded so serious on the phone"

"She showed up again Tillie, but this time she said that she wanted to take me not harm me"

"Who showed up?"

"The girl"

"Child, did she hurt you?"

"No, that's the thing. She said that she wasn't here to harm me but that she wanted to take me with her."

"Why in the world?"

"I don't know Tillie. It's really all so strange though."

"Well let's get inside and see if we can figure out who she is" she says as we all gather inside. Hadley and dad were already home and sitting in the living room watching some old home videos. It took us all back a while. For a moment we could forget about the curse and this strange girl.

It was Hadley's 4th birthday party which would make me 8. She was just getting ready to blow out her candles when I noticed something. The girl. The one from earlier. I grabbed the remote and skipped it back. Could it actually be her? I mean I'm no stranger to all this magic and weird things happening now but in one of our home videos? I played it again and sure enough it was her. She was standing to the back by a tree. I paused it on her face and asked everyone.

"Do you see it too?" I look to Tillie then to mom. "Mom, you seen her face. It's her isn't it?" I say as we are all gazing into the tv screen.

"Oh honey" mom says. "I just don't understand. She was never there before. Your father nor I know her and we've watched this video at least 100 times before. She was never in it." We turn to Tillie.

"Who is she Tillie?" I ask. Tillie steps back and goes to leave the room. "Tillie" I say while we all follow after. "Do you know her?" Tillie just stops and looks my way.

"She's my daughter." In amazement we all just stand there.

"Your daughter? How?" I say.

"Rosalie was a sweet girl. She was shy and quiet. Loved to play with her dolly"

"I don't understand Tillie. You have a daughter? How come you never told me?" she just smiles then says "She wasn't one to go out, in public ya know. She was just too shy. One evening I was on my way home but Rosalie had heard a noise out back and she went out to investigate. She thought maybe it was a small animal stuck or something. So she went to look. I had just came around the corner and was nearing the house when I saw some people running. It was getting closer to my house so naturally I was curious. I pulled on in to the drive then went to check. There was a small gathering of people so I just pushed them aside gently. When I made my way through them I saw something small lying on the ground. I knelt down for a closer look and moved the black cloth to the side so I could see what it was." Tillie stops and just closes her eyes.

"What was it Tillie?" I asked. Then a tear comes rolling down. She looks back up to us.

"It was my Rosalie." Mom gasped while squeezing dads hand.

"But what happened?" Asked Hadley.

"I looked up away from her body to a couple boys standing there laughing and throwing out names. I didn't know that my poor baby was being ridiculed by these boys, by the town. I just thought that she didn't like going out on account of her being so shy. You see those boys had lured Rosalie out by placing a kitten in the yard. They knew that my baby loved animals and she would come out to get the kitten. When she came out they beat her to death."

"That's just horrible Tillie. But why keep it inside? Rosalie should live on through you." I tell her. She smiles at me then gets up and goes back to look upon her face on the tv screen. I walk in by her. "She's beautiful Tillie. Looked to be around my age. I think her and I would have gotten along great" I say then give her a big hug.

"She was only 17 when that happened."

"What happened to the boys?"

"Oh nothing, towns folk just pushed it away. Said she probably deserved it."

"You're kidding?"

"I had my revenge though."

"Really? What did you do?" I asked.

"Let's just say that those boys will never be happy in this life, ever."

"I still don't get why she would be the one doing this though. You think you could talk to her and figure out why?"

"I don't think that's possible. You see after Rosalie's death, I had her cremated."

"What does that have to do with anything? Can't you still speak to her?"

"Well once a witch is cremated then their soul is forever gone. Removed from here."

"Really? I didn't know that."

"That's why people always burn witches my dear."

"Wow, you really do learn something everyday I guess. But still, she's speaking to me so then we can speak to her."

"We can speak to whomever that is that is inhabiting my dead child's body."

"Wait, so you're saying that that's not Rosalie then?"

"That's what I'm saying."

"But why take on her form?"

"Witches are cruel and evil. They like to do things to really get into our heads dear. Whoever it is knows that and is just trying to play games with us." After Tillie heads on home I get a visit from Azrul. He had some information on who it could be that placed this curse. Mom and dad had went on to bed and Hadley was just heading upstairs herself. He knocks on the door and I let him in.

"You're going to want to sit for what I have to tell you" he says. We go on in to the living room.

"What is it?"

"The girl you've been seeing is none other than Matilda's dead daughter" and before he could get out the name "Rosalie, I know"

"What? How"

"Tillie told us tonight about her after she showed up on one of our home videos."

"Really? We can do that?"

"What?"

"I mean, I know we can jump from time to time into another dimension but show up on homemade movies, really?"

"Azrul seriously, focus. It's not her actually, just her earthly body. So we need to know who she really is."

"It's not her? How do you know this?"

"Because Rosalie's body was cremated so it can't be her."

"Cremated. Matilda actually had her only daughter cremated? Knowing she would never see her again?"

"That's what she said. Is that all you found out?"

"Well, that was pretty magnificent ya know. I had to talk to some pretty nasty worm demons to get this information, and you don't want to know what I had to eat."

"Eat?"

"It was really disgusting. You know what worm demons eat?"

"Azrul, we have more work to do. So I hope that you made friends with these demons cause you might be visiting them again."

"Whatever it takes Gabriella. I'm not going anywhere until this is solved" he says then heads into the kitchen to grab himself a drink. I follow after.

"Really, what is your fascination with me? I mean, why feel like you need to help so much?" I ask.

"You see" he says as he leans in closer. "You my dear, are quiet amusing to me."

"Amusing? How's that?" he just smiles then begins to leave the room.

"Oh no, you don't get off that easy. Tell me Azrul, demon of darkness, Why do you feel the need to protect me so?" We gaze upon each other a moment then in walks Hadley.

"Hey guys. Any word on this video moment stealing demon, or witch, what is it exactly Gabs that's after you?" she says as she turns my way.

"I'm not sure actually."

"Well, I think she's kinda creepy" she says then takes her freshly poured cup of milk on out of the room then heads back up to her room. I look to Azrul.

"She has a point."

"What's that?"

"She is kinda creepy. I mean, she shows up whenever and now she's making an appearance on our home videos."

"You got a point" he says then we both walk back towards the living room.

"Well, if you will not be needing my assistance any more tonight my dear Gabriella, then I will be taking my leave."

"Sure, yeah absolutely" I say as I walk him over to the door.

"Again, thank you for all that you do" He places one hand on my shoulder as we both just smile.

"You know how to reach me" he says as he goes to walk out then turns back.

"Apparently" then smiles again and takes his leave. Things were getting even more mysterious lately. Why was this person trying to get to me? And why appear as Rosalie, Tillie's dead daughter? I'd have a night full of studying again I guess. Looking for any type of demon or witch that could manifest into another earthly body and also just start showing up on our videos. Found a few things that could be close but just not sure. I did read about a story in an old book that Tillie had gave me years ago for my studying. It was a witch's revenge. This witch named Serafina a Gypsy Goddess took revenge out on a family that wronged her many years ago. They took the love of her life from her. Then banished her to The Dark Forrest. She was never to return to any town or be seen by mortal man ever again or she would be hung. Serafina stayed away for many centuries until she just couldn't handle it any longer. One dark rainy night she returned into town and burned every house down with all those in it. Including women and children. Her hate grew and grew over many years. She only saw blood and revenge over the loss of her love. Afterwards she became the Revenge Goddess. All who was to seek revenge on anyone would seek out Serafina and she would make sure that revenge was definitely taken to the extreme. Could it be this Serafina that was out for me but why? What revenge would anyone be wanting on me? Other than Chrissy, I hadn't done harm to anyone. If anything, I always tried to help. I'll call out this Serafina and get some answers tonight. I placed my black candles in a circle, removed earthly garments for purity then did a blessing of my circle. Placed a dark robe on my body covered in sage and white elderberry then began my spell. It grew dark inside my room. Every candle blew out and a small tiny glow was hovering just before me. It was in my circle so was it actually evil? It couldn't be. I reached up my hand to touch it just as it moved slowly in front of me.

"Serafina" I called out. "If this is you, will you show yourself to me? Be present and trust that I only have good intentions on bringing you here." The glow hovered a few more seconds then slowly began to form into a person. A girl, sitting just in front of me. Small stature. About 10 years of age. Golden curls laying to the sides of her cheek.

"You're not Serafina?" I asked. The girl looked at me. Then her appearance began to change a bit. She grew older and curls got shorter. She now looked to be around my age maybe a little older. She stands to her feet and places her hands together, like cupping them. "Or are you?" I asked. She smiles my way then turns to scan the room. Then back to me.

"Why is it you call for me?" she asked.

"So it is you, Serafina?"

"It is. Why do you call for me?"

"I have a question."

"A question. You call me here from the darkness because you have a question?"

"Yeah" She starts to move closer to me but can't enter my circle. I notice this.

"But, you were here, close to me earlier."

"Yes, earlier I appeared as, well, not I. I appear to you first as childlike, not a mean bone in my body. Just to see if you were to harm me. Then I show to you, myself" she says.

"So, does this mean that you do, wish to do me harm then? Is this why you cannot enter my circle?"

"I" she says as she points to herself. "I do not wish to harm you. I merely want to know why it is that you have called me here. I have no reason to harm you."

"OK then, well, it seems that I have been cursed and I need to know by who and what I can do to remove this curse. Would you know anything about that?"

"You, who are you child?"

"You don't know? I just assumed that you would know everything."

"Well, I do not know. So, if you enlighten me, then maybe I can help you with your curse."

"I am Gabriella Elizabeth Delaney. Great great granddaughter of Lady Catherine Vonness" She coughs a little.

"You are Lady Vonness's granddaughter?"

"Yeah, why's that matter?"

"Well now, this will be a problem." she says as she begins to walk about my room.

"Why is this a problem?" I asked.

"Child, Lady Vonness is the one who is cursing you." Just then everything seemed to have went black. I felt like I didn't know what in the world she was talking about. "What? How can that be? I mean, are you sure?" I asked.

"Oh I'm quite sure. After all, I am the one she contacted to lay this curse upon you."

"No. I brought her back. I gave her breath again. She can't be the one. Are you absolutely positive?" I asked again.

"Yes Gabriella. Your great great grandmother has called upon me to place the most evil curse on you. One that would drive you insane."

"I don't understand. Did she say why?"

"I don't ask the why. I only do as one wishes. But I can tell you this. I felt anger, and jealously coming from deep inside her. For some reason, your grandmother is jealous of your power and wishes you nomore." I thanked the Goddess Serafina for her help. I did ask if there was anything that I could do to remove this curse and she told me that she would hold off any new spells to happen to give me some time to figuring out why Catherine has done this, but I needed to hurry cause the curse was still in effect.

I immediately went to Tillie with this. I knew that Catherine was staying with Tillie so I called her up on the phone and asked if she could meet me, only her. Not to tell anyone and I'd explain when I saw her. She did just that. I could hardly hold it all in when I saw Tillie. I first ran up and hugged her.

"What is it deary? You had me so worried on the drive over here"

"Oh Tillie, It's her"

"Who child?"

"It's Catherine that has placed the curse on me."

"Well that can't be."

"It is Tillie."

"How do you know this?" she asked.

"I was looking through one of the books you gave me years ago and I came across this Gypsy Goddess named Serafina." Tillie began shaking her head yes.

"Yeah I know Serafina. What does she have to do with this?"

"Well, apparently she is in the business of revenge you could say, and my great great grandmother called upon her to curse me."

"Are you sure? Is she sure that it's Catherine?"

"Yeah, she's sure Tillie" We both just sat there a moment both taking it all in. I turn to Tillie.

"What are we going to do?" I asked.

"Well child, we are going to stop this curse."

"We will?"

"Absolutely. We will find out why Catherine has done this and put a stop to it."

"But what if she won't answer? What if she won't stop? What then Tillie?"

"That is a bridge that we will cross when we come to it my child" We both set out to finding out why Catherine was doing this but without letting Catherine know that we know. I let Azrul know about my findings. He just dropped his head then looked back up to me.

"You knew?" I asked.

"No, but I know Catherine. I know what she will do to get whatever it is that she wants"

"Is that why you gave me the locket?"

"I figured that she would show her ugly face eventually. I did not know that it would be this soon or even at your expense, but I knew that Catherine would do something evil. That is why I gave you the locket."

"So, I can use this locket to destroy Catherine, is that it?" He starts to walk away. I follow after.

"Am I supposed to destroy Catherine with the locket? Is this how I rid myself of this curse?"

"It is one way. If it is something you wish to do. Yes, you can remove Catherine and the curse with the locket."

"But how? Won't it kill her or banish her back to wherever she came from?"

"It will. She will be removed, but this time, it will be for good" he says as I take ahold of the locket around my neck. I had just brought her back and was getting to know her. Why was she doing this though? After all, I am the one to give her life again. Why would she harm me? I had a lot of thinking to do. I was just learning all about my grandmother and getting use to her being here. Why was she doing this to me? Was it that she was jealous of me, but why? I would give her anything. I had to take my mind off these things. My wedding was fast approaching and I was actually getting a bit nervous. I love Abel with everything I have but to be sharing a home, our lives, everything. That was going to be different. I'm glad he knew about my powers and accepting it all but it didn't make it any easier. I already had things after me which meant that, after we marry, then he would too be in danger. Did I want to sentence him to a life of always looking over his shoulder? Wondering if something evil lurked in the night to come after him? I wasn't for sure if I was actually ready for that. I loved Abel more than my own life so naturally I didn't want any harm to come his way. But on another note, I could also protect him if he was always nearby. So, maybe marrying him wouldn't be that bad of an idea. I planned a get together for all us girls. Wanting to celebrate sisterhood and life in general I guess. I wanted to spend some time with mom and Hadley before the wedding day.

We all went out for bowling then grabbed some burgers from the drive in and ended our night out by the lake after a few drinks. Hadley got to try her first sip of wine. After all, she was fixing to turn 18 and graduate. She was growing up on us. I was turning 21 and about to wed my most favorite guy. I was actually able to forget about this stupid curse for a while. I even invited Catherine out with us. It was her, Tillie, mom, Hadley and one of Hadley's good friends named Emily. Emily was a sweet girl. We all liked her a lot. Shared many a laughs with this one. Her and Emily have known each other since grade school. She also knew of my powers. She's always hanging around with Hadley anymore so we figured we'd let her in on it all. Besides, she's bound to see something one day so why not tell her now? Only me, Tillie and Azrul knew of Catherine placing this curse on me. We didn't want to bother anyone else with the news. Plus, I wasn't for sure what I was going to do with her yet. I was growing to love Catherine and it broke my heart to hear of this. Maybe the reason was something that we could fix. It was worth a shot. But I didn't bother with any of it that night. Only enjoyed our girls night. No boys just us ladies out for some good ole fun. Since day one sitting in that cemetery and Finn's spirit coming to me, things have really changed a lot. I have changed so much. It was all in a good way though. If Finn never did approach me I don't know where I would be at the moment or what I'd be doing? Would I have ever gained my powers if I didn't accept him in? I wasn't sure but I'm glad I did. I was missing him and Luella actually and was wondering how they were. Had they crossed on? Were they at peace now and happy? I'm sure they were. That last Halloween night when I made my father tell of his secrets and Finn came to me. He told me that everything would be ok now. I'm just missing him a lot and was hoping to see his face. To even get his advice maybe on what to do with Catherine. But things will work out.

Us girls finished up our girls night and all went their own way. Catherine and Tillie headed to Tillie's house. Hadley and Emily headed on over to Emily's where Hadley was going to spend the night. That left mom and I by the waters. We sat and enjoyed the silence a while then mom turned to me.

"Honey, I hope you don't ever think bad of me for what your father did." I turn to her.

"Oh no mom, I never have."

"It's just, I love your father so much and I just saw only good in him. I knew he had done wrong but I wanted it all to go away. I wished every night after that that it would just go away. Wished it never happened, but it didn't. It almost tore us apart. But now that you have Abel, you under-stand what love is and that you would do absolutely anything to help them. Even if it means to lie" she just looks at me and smiles, waiting for my response. To agree and accept their wrong doing.

"Mom, dad did wrong yes, but that doesn't change anything. You guys are still my parents and I do understand love. I'll do anything for my family. Anything" We embrace one another a moment then both of us head on home. Waiting for me was none other than Abel. He was just sitting out on the front porch.

"Hey" I say as we walk on up. He stands to his feet. Mom smiles to him then walks on inside. I walk on over by him.

"What is it?" I say. I can tell something wasn't right. He just drops his head then starts to cry. I pull him closer and hug him. No words were said then he pushes back.

"I have to arrange my father's funeral tomorrow"

"Oh Abel..No. What happened?" he begins by telling me that his father had a heart attack while at work and didn't make it.

"He's at Woodland General. He's just laying there on a cold table covered with a sheet" He burys his head into my chest. I take a few moments to comfort him then I have dad to take him home and see if him or his mom needed anything. I went straight up to my room. Grabbed my grimoire and headed straight for the hospital. Figured if he was already dead then I'd go to the morgue. I find his cold dead body still laying on a table in a dark room covered with a thin white sheet. I locked the door behind me. Removed my candles from my bag and took out a sharp knife. I knew the spell that I was going to do. I had just came across it when looking for a cure for my curse. I will give blood for blood. I had brought Catherine back so I'm sure I could do something with Abel's father. Before I could begin my spell Azrul showed up.

"What are you about to do?" He asked. I just looked away and back at my book. He walks on over and grabs my arm. "Gabriella. You don't want to do this."

"Leave me" I say then throw my hand up to toss him to the side. He just keeps coming though.

"I won't let you" he says then starts blowing out the candles.

"Stop it. I'm doing this and no one is stopping me" I say. He just looks at me.

"Fine. Then I'll help. This is a powerful spell and having two will help" I just look at him.

"Suit yourself" then I turn back and start reading aloud the spell. While swaying back and forth then I punctured my hand and let the blood drip over his dead body. I say again the spell, only now my words

are not quiet English. It came out different. Guess this was what Tillie
meant by the Witch's language coming to me the stronger I got. Azrul
just watched as I went deeper and deeper into the spell. I felt the hurt
from Abel and wanted to take that away. I wanted his dad to rise from
that table, but he didn't. We stood there motionless, at first. Then the
sheet begin to slide off and his hand came out from under it. I turned
to Azrul then back to the table. His body begin to rise. He sit fully up
then looked at both of us. I didn't realize it but I was also holding onto
Azrul's hand. We both just look to our hands. I smile "It worked" then
I ran over to him.

"How are you feeling?" I asked. He kinda rubbed his head then said
"I have a splitting headache, but other than, why the hell are we down
here?" Azrul ran up to me.

"You have to make him forget" he says.

"Forget? How?"

"Just focus Gabriella. You can do it" I took a hold of Mr. Finch by
the hands and looked him in the eyes. I focused my attention and all
my energy on him.

"You will go home and go to sleep. You will wake to have had a
bad dream. You will live a long healthy life" then we all walked out
of the hospital. Before I left the parking lot I did a quick spell to make
sure all this was gone. Everyone needed to know that it was all just a
dream. Things will be back to normal. I knew then what mom had
meant by doing anything for those we love. It wasn't my dad but it was
Abel's and his heart was breaking. I couldn't have that. I had to fix it
for him, and that's what I did.

As morning came I was curious if all this had worked. I immediately
ran over to Abel's to see how he was. When I rang the doorbell no one
arrived, then, the door began to open. It was Mr. Finch. He seemed
fine. I mean, everything looked normal.

"Good morning Mr. Finch" I say.

"Good morning" he says while taking a sip of his coffee. Then turns
to point towards the stairs.

"Abel is still asleep if you're looking for him."

"I am, thanks" I say then head on up. I quietly tapped on his
bedroom door before opening it. He looked so peaceful in his slumber.

I actually didn't want to wake him. I kissed his forehead gently then just as I turned to leave the bed he reached for my hand.

"Don't go."

"Hey. I didn't want to wake you. You looked like you were sleeping so good"

"I was actually. It's been a while since I've slept that good." I smiled knowing that I had done a good thing. I fixed his broken heart and gave him hope for our future. He sits on up in his bed and rubs his eyes.

"Why you here?" he asked.

"I just wanted to see your face this morning before I headed off for work."

"That's sweet. Now come here." he says then pulls me toward him and lays a big kiss on me. I said goodbye then left for work. All seemed like it was back to normal. I stopped by the old cemetery before going to work. I felt like having a moment to myself and maybe even thanking the Gods, or whatever it was that gave Mr. Finch his life back. I went straight for my usual spot and leaned up against the old oak tree. Closed my eyes and just breathed a few deep breaths. I could feel like I was getting stronger. I felt power growing inside of me. It was nice and I was enjoying it to be honest. I was never bullied or picked on in school but I never really got "the guy" ya know. I had plenty of friends but was usually over looked by most people.

So, it was nice to be getting the attention now and having this power to make things happen. I felt sorda like a God, or should I say Goddess. I took a stroll around the graveyard just to see if I could get a feel for someone but I never did. That was kinda odd. I always feel a presense when I'm here. Maybe it was just the day. I needed to get into work so I'll check back here another day. I arrived and opened shop like usual. Had a few new packages waiting for me out back so I quickly ran them inside and began opening them. Been running low on shadow dust and black candles, also ordered some new clothing from this awesome new Wicca shop I found online. I think the clothing will be a great new addition to the shop. I started putting all my new items out on shelves when in walks Tillie. More like in runs Tillie. She comes on up to me and starts going off.

"What have you done child? Do you know the hell that you have unleashed?"

"Woah, calm down Tillie."

"Calm down?" she says as she sits then continues.

"You can't keep messing with this darkness child."

"What are you talking about?"

"Don't give me that deary. When you tap into the dark it always leaves a ripple."

"Wait, are you talking about what I did last night?"

"I'm talking about whatever it was that you did to bring forth this dark cloud over Woodland."

"Dark cloud? I only did what anyone would do with my power. You would have done the same"

"No child. I know when to stop. There are lines that we must not cross. We may be power-ful witches but that does not give the right to play God."

"Tillie, I had to."

"What exactly did you do?"

"After we all left the lake and came home I found Abel sitting on my front porch waiting for me. He told me the most horrible news. His father had passed away."

"And what did you do Gabriella?"

"I told Abel to go home and I went to see Mr. Finch at the hospital."

"You mean at the morgue?"

"I went to see Mr. Finch and I, I made things right again."

"You made things right?"

"Yes."

"How did you make things right, exactly?"

"Well, exactly. Mr. Finch is still alive."

"So, it was a false alarm then? He wasn't dead?"

"No, he WAS, dead, but, I made it to where he was no longer dead."

"You did not? Gabriella. You have been warned of entering into this dark magic. Once you start turning out these spells you will never be able to go back."

"I know Tillie, but I'm fine. I don't feel dark. I just feel like me and I made Abel happy again. He is no longer sad or hurting. You didn't see him." she comes closer to me and takes me gently by the shoulders.

"Child, what spell did you say to bring him back?" I remembered the words that I had spoken so I spoke them again to Tillie. She steps back. She begins shaking her head.

"It'll be fine really. It was a simple spell and I didn't have to sacrifice anyone."

"That's what I was afraid of my dear."

"Why? This way was so much easier. There were no killing of small animals."

"Once you no longer need to give a sacrifice of any kind, then you are already contaminated."

"Contaminated?"

"You are beginning to fill with evil. It will overcome anything else inside of you."

"I don't get it. I feel great."

"Yes, you would. You are in transition deary."

"What?"

"Your soul is being replaced with darkness. It's like the blood flowing through your veins. It is being changed over to the blackest of night. You will, in time, become what Artemis once said you would."

"NO. I am not evil. I did this out of love. I did this for Abel."

"Yes I know. You thought you were doing something good. But you cannot play God my child. We have a power to a certain degree but we are not and will not ever be GOD."

"But I only made things right. God should not have taken him anyway, not yet. Abel is not ready."

"It's not for us to decide when one is ready. Just like I couldn't fix my dear Rosalie. Sure I wanted to bring her back more than anything, but I knew I couldn't. It was merely her time. I did take my revenge out on those poor boys and I will suffer greatly I'm sure, but we cannot bring back the dead."

"Well I did, and what do you mean by those poor boys? They deserved whatever it was that you did to them. We shouldn't suffer for punishing those who do wrong."

"I know it don't seem right deary but we can't go around doing harm to those we seek. You know the rule of the witches."

"I know, do no harm and if I do, then it will come back to me threefold. But Tillie, I did no harm. It was a miracle what I done."

"No child. It was no miracle. Abel's father will take his leave and soon. And when he does, the next time will be far more greater harmful to him. His pain in death will be great."

"But that's not fair. How can I stop it?"

"You can't. It just has to play out. We will not know when it will happen, but it will happen, and it won't be too long down the road."

"I won't let it happen then. I'll put a protection spell around him. I'll protect him myself day and night if needed."

"It will not work child. Death will come for him, and death will have her prize. She will take with her whomever stands in her way." Is this all true? Did I just do more harm than good for Mr. Finch? Could I fix it? I didn't know but I would try like hell.

"I gave Catherine back her life. Does that mean that she will be taken away too?" I asked Tillie.

"That's not the same. Catherine wasn't exactly dead. Her soul was wandering, lost. You simply just gave her a body for it to go in to."

"We have to do something Tillie. At least try."

"I'll see what I got tucked away, but I won't promise anything. Like I said, death will come. And no one and I mean no one, has ever beat death." I was so worried now that something would happen to poor Mr. Finch that I just went ahead and closed up shop. I had to make sure that he was always protected. I went home and began working on many potions and charms that could help keep away this death. It may not stop her completely but it would slow her down long enough that we could find a way to get rid of her.

Twelve

My time was running out on getting everything ready for my wedding, finding a cure for this curse on me and helping Abel's dad escape death one more time. But I was Gabriella Elizabeth Delaney and I am one powerful and determined witch. I will make sure that I have the best wedding ever, remove this wretched curse and send death well on her way. I did let mom know what I had done with Abel's father and she wasn't at all pleased but she did understand and said that she too would probably have done the same thing if she were in my place and had my powers. It was starting to worry her though about the household. She thought that maybe this death would be coming for me or my little sister and she needed some reassurance that we were going to be safe. So I went about placing a protection barrier all around the house. Made my little sis a necklace with a charm on it that would ward off any demons long enough for her to make her escape. All seemed well for a few weeks to be exact.

My wedding day was fast approaching and I was hoping that all would be perfect. In fact, I'm sure it would be. Nothing had happened to any of us over the past few weeks. I hadn't had any issues with my curse either and I was hoping that maybe it was over or that the protection spell was doing its job. No mention to Catherine about this curse yet either so we did invite her to the wedding. After all, she doesn't know that we know yet. It was a beautiful Summer day. The sun was shining. Slight breeze and the smell of flowers filled the air. Everyone was starting to gather and take their seats. The excitement was really building for me. I'm sure Abel was excited and maybe even a little nervous. The wedding song began to play, *First Day of my Life* by Bright Eyes as I started to take my first steps toward this man. This man that I've known my entire life. Who saw me way before anyone else ever did. I take these steps and inch closer and closer as I look upon the smiling crowd. My mother whose eyes were filling with tears as she looked up at her baby girl moving toward the rest of her life. My little sister Hadley, whom I'm made my maid of honor. As if anyone else would ever fit that place. Then as I turn to take my stand right next to the man that I've waited for my whole life, I look on his face and see the tears rolling down. His eyes were red and he could hardly hold it all in. We take each others hands and the preacher begans the ceremony. We listened as he said a few words about us joining as one and then we each took turns saying our vows that we both took many a night to write. We continue to look into each others eyes then the words are finally spoken, after the I do's of course.

"You may now kiss the bride." We take our long awaited kiss and turn to all our family and friends as we are introduced as "Mr. and Mrs. Abel Finch" Everyone is cheering, smiling, some have tears filling their faces. We take our walk through the crowd to the back. We continued the most beautiful day I think I will ever have in my entire life by celebrating it with our loved ones. We laughed, danced, cried, ate, drank and even shared gifts. Once it was all over Abel and I headed out to our honeymoon. It was a surprise so I didn't know at the time, where we were going. I didn't care though. We could have just went back home and I would have been just as happy. I love this man, my man. I was glad that he finally picked me and that we were now actually husband and wife. That's still so weird to say out loud. Anyway, on to the honeymoon. We had a days worth of driving but once we arrived to where we were going it was all worth it. It was this charming little bed and breakfast in a small country town. He had rented out the whole bed and breakfast so we would have no interruptions from anyone.

The place was like from a magazine. So many trees in full bloom. Many kinds of flowers all around. A koi pond with small paths and walkways going through. I seriously couldn't have created it myself. It was pure heaven. We go on in and spend the next two days in our room. Just ordering room service and never leaving. On the third day we finally decided to take a walk around outside. Everything was perfect. Even the weather was perfect. It was the end of August and this place was now my new favorite. In fact, it inspired me to find a place like this on our return back home. With everything going on before the wedding Abel and I hadn't had a chance to find our forever home yet. So, after the honey-moon we took turns staying either at his house or mine. Just until we found our new home. I set out to looking right away when we returned. I was lucky to come across a small little rancher style home with some flowers around the front and back. We both seemed to like it a lot so we made them an offer. Now, we just wait. Took about two days but we did hear from the realtor, finally. They accepted our offer and said we could move in right away. Just had to sign a few papers and they would hand over our new set of keys. We were both very excited. It's moving day and I couldn't be happier. It didn't matter that it was kind of a dreary day. Cloudy and slight drizzle but we were moving on to our new adventure.

This would be the official start of our new life together. Sure we were husband and wife, but having our very own home made a world of difference. It needed very little work and I had planned on doing a lot of planting come next spring. Abel even picked out a pond set that he plans on putting in the ground for me. It was all so perfect. A couple weeks into our new home and things started getting weird. I say weird because, it wasn't scary or anything dangerous but just plain weird. Things were moving about the house. Doors were being opened but no one was there. We would leave and make sure that everything was off but on our return the tv would be playing or the kitchen light would be on. One day as I arrived home after work by myself and I began to unlock the front door, I noticed that it was already unlocked. Not open, just not locked. Maybe one of us forgot to lock up this morning, no biggie. I walk on in to find an old antique radio that Abel had from his grand-father playing. And that's not all, there was a candle lite on the dining room table. The strangest thing though, was not the radio playing or the lite candle but it was the song that was playing. It was our wedding song. First Day of my Life. That was a little too much I thought so I immediately shut it off, called Abel and asked if he had been home and did this? He had no clue what I was talking about. OK, so you wanna play? We have a ghost I guess in our home. Which was not the problem. I'm cool with ghost. Hell, I'll sit right down and have a chat if you'd like. But to start invading my home, my personal space. That was about all I could handle. Well, all I was going to handle. I took to my grimoire for some advice on ridding ghost. Found a spell that should do the trick. Brewed up a small batch of ghost be gone I like to call it then placed my circle of salt around me and said my little spell. Small odor and slight chill but no sign yet. I say it again then a dark shadow appears just before me.

"OK, So here's the thing" I tell it. "This is my home. You are welcome here as long as you know the rules. Rule number one, this is my home. Rule number two, you will at no given time touch, move and hinder us, our personal belongings in any way. Follow these rules and you will be allowed to stay. You do not, then you will be asked to leave. Got it?" I say as I look to the shadow. It just kinda circles around me then back to my front to where it then forms into a figure. It starts to shape into a person. I'm beginning to see it much clearer now. It's a girl. Looks about the age of Hadley. Beautiful face. Small frame. Short brown hair. She appears and starts to form words.

"You can see me?" she says.

"I can."

"How is that possible? No one ever has?"

"Well I'm not like others. In fact, I've seen many a dead before you."

"Then can you help me?"

"That all depends on what you mean by help?"

"I want to leave here. I want to go home."

"Home, where is that exactly?" She looks up to the sky.

"OH. You mean that home?"

"Yes. I want to go to Heaven to be with my family. I was lost from them so long ago and have been stuck here ever since."

"How did you get lost? Are you meaning by you dying?"

"No. I was already dead, but as we were traveling, going home I guess. I got pulled away by something. It was cold and dark. It pulled me here. And here is where I've been for a very long time."

"This thing that pulled you away. You say it was cold and dark? Did you see it?"

"No, it just grabbed me and as I turned to look at it, it disappeared. But I still feel it like it's still grabbing me. It just gets so cold and it's the darkest dark I've ever seen."

"Did you have a name before? Well, of course you did. I mean, what was your name?"

"My name is Elouise. My family and I were on a family vacation to see the world when we were struck by something big. It hit us in the side of the car and I think we all died. Father and mother were in the front seat with little Joe in his carseat in the middle of them. Me and my sisters Greta and Wren were all in the back. Something came and hit us. It was all so fast and quick. We didn't even know it happened. But as we were taking our leave and were following this bright light and a small voice quietly singing or humming it sounded like. Just so peaceful. As I was approaching the light I got pulled away. Everything went black for a moment like I was asleep and when I woke I was here, in this house."

"Do you know this house? Was it were you lived?" I asked.

"No. I don't recognize it at all."

"Do you know how long you've been here?"

"I don't. I don't even know where here is."

"Well you are in Woodland Grove."

"Woodland, I don't think I know it. And I don't remember it being on our way. Is it anywhere near California?"

"California? Lord no, we are on the opposite side of the world. You're in the South."

"Well, we weren't heading to the south. We were going straight for Canada. Father always wanted to visit Canada so that was the destination."

"Well now, I'm not sure why you're here but I'll try to find out." I went to the local library to dig up any info I could on my new house visitor. It didn't take long til I located an article after I entered in the names that Elouise had told me. I found something that happened just a month ago. A family who was all killed in a horrible car crash that involved a tractor trailer. It lost control and started to jack knife and went into this family's car taking them all with him. Only a month ago. But why would her ghost be here in Woodland Grove? That didn't make any sense. I contacted Tillie for some help. Her and I both went back to my place. I told Tillie about the girl and her story of how she got pulled away. We decided to call upon her again. Only this time I used an old spell. One that I had thought of and used years ago.

"Make known what I hear but cannot see. Make known and appear right in front of me." I didn't fear this ghost so I had no need for a protection spell. I'll just call her back out and maybe she'll feel safe enough to stay around this time, in the flesh, or body form, whatever. She forms in front of Tillie and I and I introduce her to Tillie. Tell her that she can trust her with anything and that she too wants to help her. I tell the girl about my new findings. That I found out that their wreck was only a month ago. She thought she had been there so much longer. In fact, years is what it felt like to her. Her family's faces were starting to fade and all she could remember was merely just her own name.

"What's happening" she asks. Tillie tries to comfort her while embracing her and letting her know that once dead you will start to forget things. Earthly things, people, faces, names. That she will slowly become a void. A shadow. Simply a ghost.

"But" I say as I look over to Tillie and then to Elouise. "We are going to try and help you move on."

"Move on?"

"Yes, we're going to try to get you to Heaven." she smiles then takes a seat.

"Now" I say to Tillie. "If you'll just help me with this, I think we can do it" Tillie is just looking at me.

"Do what child?" she says quietly.

"You and I are going to free her from this place. It seems as if her soul is simply trapped in this house."

"She is trapped Gabriella but we do not know why she is trapped. Nor do we know who has trapped her here."

"What are you trying to say Tillie?"

"Someone could have trapped her here for a good reason child. A spirit can appear to you however it likes." Tillie says as she takes me to the side. We are both sorda quietly talking in hopes that Elouise won't hear us.

"Tillie, I'm sure it will be fine. And besides I don't want her trapped inside my house."

"No, you wouldn't would you. Very well" she says as we gather back into the same room. "Let us begin." Tillie says and takes ahold of my hand. We stand just before Elouise both chanting the same spell to free her from this place. We stand our ground and say it once more. Just then the girl falls to the floor and a dark cold presence appears before us. A lady dressed in all black. Long hair passed her bottom flowing in the wind. Such charming face and a smile that made you feel at peace. I look over to Tillie then as if I'm asking who is she, Tillie just shrugs an I don't know. We both look back to the woman.

"You have meddled where you don't belong for way too long Gabriella." she says.

"How do you know me?"

"I know everyone." she says.

"And who are you?"

"I am someone that you do not want to be meeting, not any time soon." Tillie then realizes and grabs me tightly by the hand.

"She's death child." she says. I swallow hard then stand firm. I knew I had to show no fear to her.

"So you are her? I have heard many things of you."

"I'm sure not all good I'm afraid." she says.

"No. Nothing about death is good."

"Well I wouldn't say that. You see, we need death to happen. It's the way of life. You can't keep on going forever so that's where I come in. I take you to a better place."

"A better place? What about Mr. Finch?"

"Yes about that. You took something that didn't belong to you Gabriella. And I'm afraid that I'll have to take it back."

"He wasn't ready. You can take him when he's old and has lived a long life with his family and grandkids."

"I'm afraid it don't all work out that way. Not all are meant to live this long life. Some are ready to go to their final resting place way before others. It's how it must be."

"Does it though? Have to be like that? You're death. You're choosing who and when you take them. Why not wait?"

"Oh I don't chose young one. I take, yes. But I am not the one who choses."

"Then who?" I ask as she looks up to the sky.

"Then I'll pray to God for Abel's father. Is that what I have to do?" She just shrugs her shoulders.

"If you wish, but his name is still written down."

"Then erase it."

"It doesn't work that way." she says. Tillie then stops me.

"Dear, pick your battles. This is one you will not win. Let's just focus on this girl." she says.

"Fine." I say then turn back. I look to the girl on the ground then back to death.

"Is she on your list?" I ask.

"She is not."

"Then why are you here? Why was she taken in the crash?"

"It was a mistake. Her family had died but she was to survive."

"Then why did she die?"

"She was pulled away to keep the balance."

"What balance? What are you talking about?" I asked.

"You see child, when you brought Mr. Finch back to this earth then death had to take another in his place." My heart sank.

"You mean, It's my fault that she's dead?" Death looks upon us and shakes her head yes.

"No, then I'll fix it" Tillie comes closer.

"Oh child, you can't can't fix everything. You are going to have to let this one go I'm afraid" Death moves in closer to us.

"She's right. Now you can chose."

"Chose?"

"Yes, this girl or Mr. Finch? Chose." I just look to the poor girl lying motionless on the floor and I can picture Abel and his father out in his back yard throwing ball. They loved to throw ball and play sports together. This was all my fault. Tillie was starting to make sense on what she was saying by me playing God. I was seeing for the first, my actions were not coming out very good at all. I look to Tillie then to death. I turned to walk away then said, with my back to them.

"Take her" and I left the room. It was a difficult decision but I knew that I couldn't handle seeing Abel so heart broken again over his father's death. I know it will one day happen, but at least I could buy more time. Death took with her the young girl and left my home that night. I cried as I layed my head in Tillie's lap.

"What have I done Tillie? I never wanted to hurt anyone?"

"I know child, I know." she said as she stroked my hair. Just then Abel comes home. He finds us still on my couch as Tillie is comforting me.

"What did I miss?" he says. Tillie gets up and gathers her purse.

"I'll leave the two of you to talk." she says then heads on out. I begin telling Abel of my horrible actions. Even that his father had passed away and how I brought him back. He was confused and hurt. Somewhat grateful for what I had done but still very hurt by me doing this and not telling him about it when it had happened. Or even asked his opinion on if I should do it or not. He at least wanted the choice. I told him everything even about the curse that has been placed upon me. He wanted no more secrets. He was grateful that I was finally honest but he was still so hurt by all the secrets and lies. He left to spend the night with his folks. He needed some time alone to think. In a way, I guess the curse was still working its power on me cause she said that I would know pain and suffering and she was right.

Although I just married the man of my dreams and we had found our dream home, things were still spinning out of control. All the good that I was doing was just turning around to become something evil. I wasn't for sure if I had been doing the right things after all. All I knew is that I needed to protect my loved ones and I needed to remove this curse from me. I was going to go straight to Catherine about it. If it was really her that has done this, then I wanted answers. I was waiting no longer. I went straight over to Tillie's as soon as I woke. I was ready to find out why Catherine was doing this to me. They were both already up and sitting on the front porch. I go on up to Catherine and start demanding answers.

"Why are you doing this?" I asked. "Tell me why exactly you feel that you need to hurt me so, after I did everything in my power to bring you back?" I say to her and stand and wait her response. She lowers her head then stands to her feet.

"I see." she says as she starts to walk inside.

"Wait. You can't just leave. I need to know why?" I say and wait again for her reply. I could tell that Tillie was anxious as well for a response. We all stand there, waiting when Catherine then turns back to me.

"Because you have everything. Everything that I never had, and everything that I tried so hard to get. It all just falls into your lap."

"Everything? I have worked for what I have. And I would do anything to help you get all that you wanted. All you would have had to do was ask. Why place a curse?"

"Because it is the only way. Your power is growing and I have to stop that?"

"But why? You are my grandmother. You should be happy for me. Instead you set out to harm me."

"Family, yes. I am your bloodline. Your start you might say. In fact, I am the reason for your power. But you do not respect me for that. You move on growing stronger every day. You and Tillie go through your lessons. Do you ever think to consider me? Do you care that I might be affected by all this power that you are craving?"

"Consider you? What would my powers have to do with you? You may have started me on my journey but I am the reason for my growth. I am the one who let in all this power and I'm the one that decided on taking this journey. You were nowhere in sight. Tillie is who showed up. Tillie is who helped me understand who I was and she is the one who taught me how to grow in my powers."

"Yes, Tillie, Matilda. I should thank you, shouldn't I? You have awaken this young heart to her own enlighten spiritual path. You have pushed her to keep going. It is you Matilda that maybe I should have cursed to begin with. But instead I chose to place this curse on Gabriella. Hoping that she would learn her lesson and stop with all this nonsense." Tillie comes closer to Catherine.

"You are a disgrace to the witch name. You had a good start and became something huge yourself, but you chose to go the wrong way Catherine. You chose the darkness and it over took you. It consumed you to the point where you no longer valued human life."

"I valued human life. Just not in the way that you do. I value myself first."

"And it shows" I say.

"You young child, have so much more to learn about your powers. You think you are truly who you are? You can be so much more."

"I don't want to be more. I'm happy with who I am, and my powers are just fine. I am stronger than most. I held one of the most powerful demons in his place. Someone who yourself could not even contain."

"Yes Azrul. How's that going?" she asked.

"It's going just fine. He is far better of a person than yourself actually." I say to her.

"Is he? Has he told you of his true reason to why he is always around and helping you?"

"He has no true reason. He just feels the need to protect me for some reason."

"You would think that wouldn't you?" she asked.

"Stop trying to turn this around to him. This is about you and why you feel the need to put a curse on me."

"I placed this curse to slow you down a bit."

"Slow me down?"

"As I said before, you are getting way too powerful for your own good. Artemis has saw great things in his time and he has foretold of you letting in the darkness and becoming evil. I'm only doing what any other great witch would do" Just then Tillie chimes in.

"Artemis was a fool. I saw his ramblings and Gabriella is nothing like he has described. She has way too much good in her. And besides, you have placed this curse out of jealously. For your own good. Not for the good of the witches. Face it Catherine, you want her beauty, her power, her life. You are trying to take it just as you have taken all those other poor souls." Catherine just laughs a little then begins to walk off the porch, but turns back to us and says "Pain and suffering like you've never known" while looking me straight in my eyes. Then takes her leave.

"Tillie she has to be stopped."

"I know child, but how we do it will be somewhat difficult. Catherine is no ordinary witch. She will see us coming before we get there."

"There has to be a way. Serafina gave us a little time to figure this out, and that's what we're going to do" I set out on learning all I could about Catherine. Her history. What makes her tick and how to exact this revenge without her knowing ahead of time. I headed back home and cleaned up a bit. Trying to get my mind off all this. I needed for Abel to be ok with everything. He had to see why I had kept those secrets. He knew of my powers for quite some time now and was very accepting of it all. I explained to him that he would have done the same thing if he were in my place. I just didn't want to see him in pain.

After I finished cleaning up I headed on to bed. I was hoping that Abel would be back home in the morning. I'll get a good night's rest then begin my day anew. Morning came, and no Abel. I immediately got dressed and began my day. I couldn't focus too hard on this. He just needed some time and he'll be back home in a few days, I was hoping anyways. Went on in to the shop to find Abel inside talking to mom.

"Good morning" I say as I enter. They're both sitting at the table having a cup of coffee and they both turn my way.

"Morning dear" mom says. Abel then stands to his feet and leans in to give me a kiss on my cheek.

"Good morning" he says then sits back down.

"Good morning. What's going on? Why here so early?" I ask.

"Just wanted to get my day going. I came in and Abel was already in here." mom says.

"Really?" I say then look his way.

"Yeah, I was hoping that we could talk."

"Talk? Of course, about what?"

"Well, I was kind of a jerk. Just taking off like that. I had some time to think and I do understand why you done what you did. I do wish that, in the future, if something like this happens again, I'd like for you to be honest with me. Tell me up front, don't wait."

"Yeah absolutely" I say as I move in closer to give him a hug. We embrace one another then the door chimes. In walks Catherine. Yep, she comes strolling in as if none of this ever took place.

"Why are you here? If you haven't figured out by now, you are no longer welcome" I say to her. Mom seems puzzled.

"Honey, why would you say that?" she asked me.

"Mom, Catherine is the one who has cursed me."

"Catherine? Are you sure?"

"A hundred percent."

"But how did you find out?"

"I have my ways" I say then begin leading Catherine to the door.

"I'll leave Gabriella, but just know that I am still around" she says then heads on out. Abel walks up to me.

"What are you going to do? Is there a way to remove the curse now that you know who it is?" he asked.

"That's what I'm working on. I do have some things in place. There are a few ways that I can rid this curse and her, but that means that she will no longer be here. And I'm just not sure that I'm ready to do that. After all she is my great great grandmother and I've been learning so much about our family line. I just can't believe that it is her that is doing this" We spent the day as normal as we could. Customers coming and going. Then closing up by night time. As I'm locking the door I turn to Abel "Will you be coming home tonight?" I asked. He smiles my way and nods his head yes. I smile back and we gather back at the house. I had a dream that night with Catherine in it. It was her sitting by the fire just like when I had first saw her. She was rocking and humming while sewing on a blanket. The man walks in again and they began laughing and dancing. Everything moved slowly and began to get slower. Almost to a stop when Catherine turns to me and her eyes turn dark and cold. It's like she was looking straight at me. She's smiling and dancing when suddenly she turns back around, and this time the man's face has changed. It's Abel. He looks my way and he too is smiling as they embrace one another and kiss deeply. I then wake up and sit up in my bed. I look over to Abel. What did this mean? Was it Catherine? Did she invade my dream and was it her way of saying that she was going to come after Abel? I too can play those games though. I went right to placing a protection spell around him and even taught him a chant to say just in case he were to encounter evil doings. I opened up my grimoire and began reading pages, pages that before I could not understand. The words were so clear now. As my power grew so did my understanding of our witch language. And what perfect time? I could use the new spells that I could now read to rid us of this evil curse and, if needed, Catherine too.

Thirteen

I put all my attention in on conjuring up all that I needed to put an end to all this evil that Catherine has placed upon us. Things were going smoothly over the next few days. No sign of Catherine or anything else for that matter. Took a week off from work and left the shop in mom's hands for a while so I could dig deeper into my reading and learning all that I could. I was preparing myself for one of the hardest fights I'd have to do. I hoped that Catherine would have a change of heart and maybe just stop this curse herself, but unfortunately she didn't. No worries. Tillie, Azrul and I were gathering up all that we needed so that this night would go off as smooth as possible. I found a spell that would banish her to the forbidden forest. A place where a witches' soul will be lost and wander forever. In hopes that, one day we could bring her back out and hopefully she would see things differently then. After all, she is family and I wanted to help and protect as much family as I could. I understood why Catherine was doing this. I get that she was a jealous soul and longed for beauty beyond compare her whole life, but I only hoped that blood would make her see things different. She needed to see that she has family that is here and is willing to help her in any way. This banishment would put a stop to this curse and would also hold her at bay for however long I needed. She would be stuck in the forbidden forest until I released her. In which, I had no intentions until I knew that all around me was safe from her grasp. Even if it meant that she would no longer be in our lives. Then that was a price I was willing to pay.

A full moon was approaching and everything was in place. We would do this spell in the cemetery. A place were our powers will be at full charge and with the full moon helping us, we should have no problems in containing Catherine and going through with this spell. We had to get her there though. That did come as a little snag. But I did have a plan. I planned on Azrul getting her to meet him at the cemetery so they could talk. That way they would have privacy. I did a small chant to shield Tillie and I. We needed Catherine to think that they were alone. She would be able to feel us. So this spell would hide Tillie and I long enough for her to get into the cemetery and make her way over to our circle. A circle that we made of black spider dust, salt and demons blood. A circle to hold the strongest of witch's. Everything is going according to plan. Azrul shows up right on time with Catherine right behind him. They come strolling through casually chatting as Tille and I are standing and waiting behind a tall gravestone. He stops her suddenly right in the circle but she doesn't notice. She still only believes that he really just wants to talk with her. He was telling her how he felt that all this between her and I was just ridiculous. We were family and she should just drop all this non sense so we could get back to the way it was before. But she would only laugh.

"Non sense" she says.

"It is all non sense, but you should understand why. Why I am and will continue to go through with this curse. Gabriella Elizabeth Finch is growing way too strong in her powers. She will be able to rid all evil if she wanted soon. And me, for that matter."

"Yes but, you, you are her blood. The one that she spent many a nights working hard to finding a spell to bring you back. Why would you have to worry about her doing anything to you? I mean, if you just loved her then she would not wish to do you harm."

"Love? What is that exactly? One cannot have love and keep it. It just gets ripped away from your hands."

"Love is what Gabriella has. She is not evil. She is trusting and kind. She is nothing that Artemis has said her to be."

"Not now, but she will be. Look at the things she has already done."

"You mean help all those around her? She only tries too hard to make everything perfect, that is her down fall."

"Help? Was it helping Chrissy to take her life and give it to you? And what about Mr. Finch? You know how death works. He will be taken and the next time will be far greater painful than he could imagine. I don't see that she is really helping, do you?" I had had just about all that I could handle. It was time for Tillie and I to make our appearance. We emerge from behind the gravestone. Catherine turns to us.

"I kind of figured that something was up. And good job Gabriella on keeping you two hidden. I am impressed" she says as we walk closer but stay just outside the circle. She laughs at us.

"Well, now you've got me here. What are you planning on doing with me? You know this circle will not hold me long. So whatever it is, I suggest you get to doing it my dears." Azrul joins closer to Tillie and I and we began our chant. We say it twice with no effect but by the third time the winds begin to blow and the night gets darker. Spirits from the graves are circling from above. She stands with her smug look believing that she will make it out of this unharmed. Not knowing that this spell is different. Before arriving at the cemetery that night I called upon death one more time. I made her a little offer. I would help her with uping the talley on her souls and give her one that she has longed for quite some time. A witch's soul is hard to get. They are protected by magic and usually death cannot touch. Having this soul will give death more power. Power like she's never known before. She will reap for many many years. So while saying our little chant a few more times we were joined by death herself. She is more than willing to help us out with Catherine. You see Catherine is filled with so many other souls. So not only will her soul be ever so gratifying already. Death will be able to take all those lost souls that once belonged to her. Death stands close by our sides as we say one final time this chant. We watch Catherine's face change. She then began to realize that this was going to happen. This was going to finally stop her and that she couldn't do anything to stop it. After all, we had death on our side and who could fight with death? The darkness from inside starts to make its way out of Catherine. She tries to pull it back but she is powerless. Death consumes all that was inside and Catherine's lifeless body falls to the ground. We stand quiet a moment. I look over to death as she smiles.

"It is done." she says then vanishes into the night. I immediately look to Tillie.

"It worked. It really worked." she shakes her head yes. Azrul himself is also amazed.

"You did it." he says.

"We did it." I tell him.

"All of us did this. Together we put our powers in and we finally put a stop to Catherine. Lady Vonness will no longer be a worry for young beautiful souls." We take in a few moments of happiness and just could not believe that our spell actually worked. Catherine wasn't exactly gone for good. Death consumed all those lost souls from inside. The ones that Catherine took over the years. She took in Catherine's but only to carry her to the forbidden forest where she will stay. She'll be there wandering and suffering until I decide to bring her back. If I ever do decide to that is. The curse was finally gone. I could move on from this horrible nightmare. I didn't have to worry about something tragic happening to me or my loved ones now. And I did this without letting in any darkness. It was all just my natural powers. Maybe I would survive this after all. For years, after hearing of this Artemis and how he foretold of me being evil, that's all I thought of. Always wondering if I was slowly becoming evil. Everything I done was always questioned, by me. I hated that I took poor Chrissy's life but that was the only way to bring my great great grandmother back. If I had known that all this would happen, would I still have done it? Probably. I never regret any of the good times that I had with Catherine. I did learn so much from her and our bloodline. I will give it some time to let her think it all over then maybe one day I'll make that decision to try and bring her back one more time. But if I do then there will be barriers and restrictions for a long time just to be safe. I was now ready to move forward with somewhat of a normal life. Hopefully we could skip on all the drama and darkness for a little bit anyway. After all, I had a new home and husband to tend to. I was now Mrs. Gabriella Elizabeth Finch. Wow, that still sounds weird but I'm getting use to it. I deserved to be happy for a while and happy is what I tend to be.

Weeks passed with no signs of anything evil. No signs of Catherine trying to return. How could she though? This was a power that even Lady Vonness could not fight. She will stay in The Forbidden Forest until I decide to give her another chance. And only I could bring her back. I liked that. It helped me to feel at ease knowing that she wouldn't be popping up in the near future to do harm to any of us. Life was moving along rather nicely actually. I was getting the hang of this married life and still had time for the magic shop and other family activities. Hadley had been seeing a new guy and it seemed to be getting pretty serious. She worked part time at the shop and usually when she was there you would also see Owen Creed. Nice young man. A couple years older than Hadley but they seem to hit it off really well. He took a great liking to Abel as well and was always around trying to get him to do things or go out. I didn't mind. It gave me a little me time and let him enjoy some of his own time as well. You know, not to be getting too much wifey time. Everything was going great. So of course I'm just here waiting and wondering for something big to happen. We just never get this much quiet time. Some sort of evil is bound to show its ugly head soon, and boy does it. Something huge was headed straight for Woodland Grove and right to Bennington Ave. It practically walks right up to my door. But that's a story for another time. A story in which we shall dig deeper into this madness, this darkness that we call evil and try to contain its sanity for the time being. Right now, I am going to enjoy my cup of mocha coffee and flip through my Edgar Allan Poe novel. And just be normal for this day. For these last few hours of peace, quiet and tranquility.

Printed in the United States
by Baker & Taylor Publisher Services